Porcine Pranks at St. Anne's

Emily Gulley

Copyright © 2023 Emily Gulley

The moral right of the author has been asserted.

Apart from any fair dealing for the purposes of research or private study, or criticism or review, as permitted under the Copyright, Designs and Patents Act 1988, this publication may only be reproduced, stored or transmitted, in any form or by any means, with the prior permission in writing of the publishers, or in the case of reprographic reproduction in accordance with the terms of licences issued by the Copyright Licensing Agency. Enquiries concerning reproduction outside those terms should be sent to the publishers.

This is a work of fiction. Names, characters, businesses, places, events and incidents are either the products of the author's imagination or used in a fictitious manner. Any resemblance to actual persons, living or dead, or actual events is purely coincidental.

Matador
Unit E2 Airfield Business Park,
Harrison Road, Market Harborough,
Leicestershire. LE16 7UL
Tel: 0116 2792299
Email: books@troubador.co.uk
Web: www.troubador.co.uk/matador
Twitter: @matadorbooks

ISBN 978 1805140 283

British Library Cataloguing in Publication Data.
A catalogue record for this book is available from the British Library.

Printed and bound in Great Britain by 4edge Limited
Typeset in 11pt Cambria by Troubador Publishing Ltd, Leicester, UK

Matador is an imprint of Troubador Publishing Ltd

*For Grandilarious,
Lots of love and hugs
from Emilarious*

Contents

Character List	vii
New Arrivals	1
Elaine Wilson	12
Wang Li's Story	21
A Secret Shared	31
Nan Makes an Enemy	38
Trouble for the First Form	46
A Plague on Miss Winter	60
Bobby Joins the French class	69
Miss Winter is a Nuisance	80
Discovery!	87
The Telegram	100
Elaine's Second Chance	112
A Trial and a Tea	124
A Discussion Over Dinner	131
Mamzelle and the Ghost of St Anne's	136
Two Pieces of good News	151
Leonora on the Case	158

A Lacrosse Match	163
An Unpleasant Encounter	174
A Plan	189
A Pig in a Thunderstorm	196
Mamzelle's Niece	212
A Midnight Feast	222
Snowballs and Philosophy	231
Until Next Term	248
Maps, plans and glossary…	253
First form timetable	256
Plan 1	257
Plan 2	258
Plan 3	259
Plan 4	260
Glossary	261
About the author	270

Character List

First Formers:

In Miss Porter's house:

Nan Miller

Poppy Pearson

Barbara Wofflespoon

Zhang Wang Li

Beryl Forsyth

Daisy-May Brain

Elaine Wilson

(Bobby the Pig)

In Miss Spark's House:

Leonora Jameson

Millicent Appleby

Flora

Agnes

Sixth Formers:
Amrita Kaur Anand- Games Captain

Isobel Harding- Head Girl

Teachers and staff:
Miss Montagu- Headmistress and Latin mistress

Miss Rowan- 2nd form mistress and deputy head

Miss Porter- 1st form mistress and Geography mistress

Mamzelle Meuhourat- French mistress

Miss Sparks- Science mistress

Miss Whyte- Art and Sewing mistress

Miss Knight- Games mistress

Miss Layton- Music mistress

Miss Winter- Drama mistress

Matron Bigley

Cook

Mary the palourmaid

Annie the kitchenmaid

Fred

Parents and People:
Phil Miller

Mr. Miller

Mrs. Miller

Character List

Professor Wofflespoon
Mr. Zhang (Zhang Chen)
Mrs. Zhang (Tang Zhi Ruo)
Miss. Amelia Blake

1

New Arrivals

Nan Miller collected her things together and prepared to disembark from the train. The journey had been relatively uneventful as it was not a busy day and she had had the carriage to herself. She had been glad of that in a way, as it enabled her to collect her thoughts, which were many as this was to be her first term at boarding school. Up until now she had attended the local village school where she knew everyone, and everyone knew her. Things were going to be very different now.

These musings were interrupted by a piercing whistle as the train came to a halting stop. Looking out of the window Nan saw an array of red brick houses framed by enticing dark woods. This was as far as the train went. The next step was to board a bus that would take them to the village of Hillesley from whence they could walk to St Anne's.

Just as Nan was debating dubiously what was to be done about the outsize trunk about the size of a small house which constituted her wardrobe, a friendly porter appeared.

'You for St Anne's?' he enquired genially, taking in the gingham dress and dark green blazer which were the uniform of that illustrious school.

Nan nodded, and gave him a shy smile, too overwhelmed to speak. The porter however needed no encouragement and chatted away merrily as the two of them crossed the platform, Nan marveling at the glistening black engine as it sat there cooling off from its recent exhaustion.

'Beautiful ain't she?' remarked the porter, following the girl's gaze. 'I've got the best job in the world I have.'

'What about the train driver?' asked Nan timidly. 'Hasn't he got the best job?'

'He's got a hot job, and no mistake,' commented the porter, 'But he doesn't get to see the train, does he? I gets to see all sorts of trains.'

Nan agreed doubtfully and watched as he stowed her trunk safely in the shining green and cream charabanc that was to convey her to school. Then with a tip of the cap he was gone, and Nan climbed up into the charabanc, marveling at how many St Anne's girls there

New Arrivals

had been on the train. She hadn't seen a single one, but she supposed they had all got on gradually at each stop.

Momentarily taken aback at the number of new faces, Nan stood there rooted to the spot, her face flushing as she noticed they were all staring at her. Hard, curious, appraising stares which did nothing to make the first former feel welcome.

Then just when she felt she could stand it no longer her gaze fell upon a girl of about her own age with a thick plait of blond hair and wide blue eyes. The girl was looking her in the eyes, an almost pleading expression on her face and her right hand was gently tapping the empty seat beside her.

Grinning infectiously, Nan made her way through the bus full of new faces and took the seat offered to her with a little sigh of relief. To her surprise, she found that her knees were shaking.

The girl with the plait smiled at her and she smiled back gratefully. The bus gave a sudden lurch, and they were off.

To her annoyance Nan found that she was still an object of curiosity to a lot of the girls on board and she found herself staring out of the window to avoid their stares.

The countryside flashed past and before long they were there. The bus stopped on the outskirts of the village and trunks were unloaded and given into the care of a funny little man with a wild mass of white hair escaping out of a tweed cap and gnarled features. He in turn loaded them onto a ramshackle looking truck with an air of a cart about it, and the girls were left free to walk to the school.

It was only when they had descended from the bus and dissipated somewhat that the girl spoke.

'I'm Poppy Pearson,' she said, extending a hand.

'I'm Nan Miller,' replied Nan, shaking it firmly.

'I'm new,' said Poppy, 'And I'm guessing you are too?'

'Yes,' admitted Nan, then, looking round her, 'I say, shouldn't we have stuck with the others, I don't know the way to the school from here.'

'Ah, but I do,' grinned Poppy. 'It's quite simple, we just follow this path through the wood,' she added, gesturing to a narrow dirt track winding off through the sun-streaked trees.

'How do you know all this?' asked Nan, bewildered. Poppy exuded an air of quiet confidence that made Nan quite ready to believe she had been at the school for years.

'It's quite simple,' said Poppy modestly, 'I've just visited the school with my aunt and made sure I'm familiar with everything because you know, I really don't like new things,' she confided, smiling.

The charabanc let out a loud bang and lurched off again to collect the next trainful of girls. Nan and Poppy waved to the driver before setting off through the wood.

New Arrivals

It was a beautiful day, warm and sunny with a refreshing breeze. The light shone through the many leaves, picking out radiant greens and casting dappled shadows onto the dry earth path.

The light reflected in Nan's dark eyes and made her dark skin glow. Her hair stood out from her round face like a halo.

Suddenly she stopped and put a startled hand to her mouth. 'What was that?' she cried, 'in your bag?'

Poppy stopped too and looked at Nan as though she were reading her. From her satchel there came the most peculiar grunting and snuffling noises.

'Well,' she said at last, 'I like your face, so I'll tell you. But you must promise not to tell a soul.'

Nan nodded mutely.

Poppy reached inside her bag and drew out a small pale pink something that wriggled in her arms.

'She's a piglet', said Poppy, kissing her nose lovingly. 'Her name is Bobby and she's mine. You see I live on a farm and just before the end of the summer hols, our sow had a litter of five piglets. Bobby was the runt so I got to keep her, and obviously I couldn't face leaving her for so long so soon after getting her, so I took her along with me.' So saying, Poppy gently replaced the squirming piglet in her bag, arranging the top carefully to hide her head.

Nan was staring at her friend in amazement.

'Where will you keep her?' She asked at last.

'There's sure to be an outhouse or a box room handy,' opined Poppy confidently, 'A box room would be better as I normally sleep with her, and she isn't used to being far from me.'

'And what about food?'

'Oh, we can easily manage that,' replied Poppy breezily, setting off briskly again, 'We'll smuggle something off the table and wrap it in a handkerchief for her.'

'We?' questioned Nan astutely.

'You will help, won't you?' queried Poppy looking suddenly alarmed.

'I suppose so,' said Nan slowly. She secretly thought Bobby very cute and would be delighted to see more of her but she wasn't sure she wanted Poppy to know just how enthusiastic she was yet; she didn't want to get herself in too deep.

Just then she heard a gasp from Poppy and looked up to see that they had reached the school and it was just visible. Framed by the straggling branches of the trees, was a massive block of imposing Victorian red brick architecture sitting in a small lake of gravel. At its base swarmed girls sporting the distinctive uniform, parents in flashy sports cars and teachers attempting to restore some kind of order.

'Where do we go?' asked Nan suddenly shy of the mass of unknown people.

'Well,' said Poppy, taking control, 'I suppose we had better make our way to our house. I say I hope we're in the same one. I'm in Miss Porter's, what about you?'

Nan carefully extracted a scrap of paper from her blazer pocket on which was printed the name of her form mistress and house mistress. They were both the same; Miss Porter.

'Oh yes, she is the first form mistress,' commented Poppy, peering over her shoulder, 'Well come on. We want plenty of time to unpack before tea.'

The two set off across the gravel drive, Poppy leading the way. Together they skirted around the side of the school and found themselves at the top of a large grassy bank surveying a view across an expanse of lawn to a patchwork of fields in the distance. To the left soared the crumbling ruins of Hillesley Castle and next door to St Anne's the many-paned windows of St Becket's school for boys glistened in the late afternoon sun.

Skirting the edge of the immaculate lawn was a raised path, which, hugging the edge of the trees, wound down to a small cluster of houses.

On reaching the houses, Poppy stopped, suddenly uncertain.

'I'm not sure which one it is,' she admitted, rubbing her nose in a vexed manner.

'Well, I am,' said Nan unexpectedly, 'it's the second one.

Poppy's eyes widened, 'How?' she began.

Nan grinned and, seizing her arm, led her up to the house, 'it says on the gate,' she pointed out smilingly.

'So it does,' chuckled Poppy.

It was a very pretty whitewashed Georgian house with a small front garden and sheltered porch. The door was wide open and from within came the sound of voices.

Nan and Poppy entered and found themselves in a small hall with a polished wooden floor in which was a desk. Behind the desk was a large woman wearing a plain dress and nurse's watch, her hair in a small bun at the back of her neck. When her eyes fell on the two girls she emitted a low clucking in the back of her throat like a mother hen.

'Well, that's two more to tick off the list,' she remarked suiting the action to the word, 'names please?'

'Nan Miller'

'Poppy Pearson'

'Got your health certificates?' she asked, a glint in her eye, 'If not it's quarantine for you.'

The two health certificates were hastily handed over. Matron eyed them closely as if doubting their authenticity and then placed them on a shelf behind her and beamed at the two first formers.

'I'm Matron Bigley of Miss Porter's,' she said warmly, extending a podgy hand to each of them.

New Arrivals

'I believe your trunks have already been brought up, so you can unpack straight away. There were supposed to be eight of you this term but Mamzelle's niece is ill and can't join us yet, so there's an extra bed. The first form dormitory is on the first floor on your right,' explained Matron briskly, indicating a set of stairs off the hall.

'Oh, and by the way' she added in what seemed to Nan a faintly menacing tone as both girls moved towards the stairs, 'I hope you can both darn. Matching thread would be helpful...'

With these cryptic remarks she returned to her tasks and Poppy and Nan fled gratefully up the stairs.

'I can't believe she didn't see Bobby!' exclaimed Nan, stifling a giggle.

'Shh!' reprimanded Poppy sternly, 'there may be more of us'

The first form dormitory, however, was empty and there were no signs of any other girls having arrived except for the bed nearest the door on the right-hand side. There was a coat thrown across it and the bedside table was littered with trinkets and sweet wrappers. Nan marveled that anyone could make so much mess within five minutes of arriving.

The room itself was light and airy with two windows at the far end overlooking a colourful flower garden which appeared to be shared by the two neighbouring houses. Each bed had a pale floral bedspread, a small wooden bedside cabinet and a chest at the end of the bed for clothes. At the far end of the room underneath the windows were four washbasins and a mirror. A door to the right led to a bathroom.

'Which bed do you want?' asked Poppy.

'Let's go next to the window,' suggested Nan, opening her bag and starting to unpack.

Poppy plonked her blazer across the bed next to Nan's and looked about her. She saw that there were two trunks next to the door. Crossing the room she read the labels, 'These are ours. Golly, it's going to take ages to unpack all this lot. And I did want to find somewhere to keep Bobby before tea. Blow!'

'You go,' urged Nan, 'I'll get started with this, I'm quick at unpacking.' Then, as Poppy hesitated, 'Go on, the others could arrive any minute.'

So Poppy sped off. She toured the first floor but only found a small box room that was obviously in use and would soon house the girls' trunks. She was resigning herself to slipping past Matron to search the garden when halfway down the stairs she spotted another small staircase almost hidden by the curve of the wall. She climbed up the narrow steps, which veered to the left and found herself face to face with a giant wooden door with an old-fashioned lock. The key was hanging on a nail next to the door and was thick with dust. Excited,

New Arrivals

Poppy took up the key and fitted it into the lock. It turned eventually but was very stiff. Poppy's spirits rose, that must mean that no one had used it in ages, making it the perfect hiding place. Inside was a small sparsely furnished room with a window overlooking the wood. It smelled dreadfully musty, so Poppy opened the window. Then she took out Bobby and made her comfortable on a rug in the corner. The little piglet curled up quite happily and went to sleep. Smiling fondly, Poppy closed the door, locked it and dropped the key into her pocket.

Bursting to tell Nan her news she made her way back to the first form dormitory. Flinging open the door she had to swallow her words as she saw that Nan was not alone.

The others had arrived.

2

Elaine Wilson

'Hello,' said a long thin girl stepping forward, 'You must be Poppy Pearson. Nan was just telling us about you. My name's Barbara Wofflespoon by the way.'

'Oh hullo,' said Poppy, studying the girl closely. She had short dark hair in two bunches and large round glasses framing grey green eyes.

'I suppose you think I'm terribly forward' she continued, perching on a nearby trunk, 'But you see my father's one of the housemasters at St Becket's, so I've lived here all my life'

'Goodness,' said Poppy, surprised, 'Well you'll be jolly useful to have around then, I bet you know all there is to know.'

'Well, I have rather made it my business,' admitted

Barbara, before saying hurriedly, 'Anyway, Introductions. This here is Beryl Forsyth...'

A petite girl with thick golden curls and a smattering of freckles stepped forward.

'Zhang Wang-Li...'

The Chinese girl bowed her head slightly in greeting. She was also petite with thick black hair tied tightly back and a pale spotless face, her eyes a beautiful almond shape.

'And Daisy-May Brain.'

Daisy-May was a stocky girl with a determined look in her eye and a styled bob of brown hair. She had an air of stolid dependability about her.

'So that's six of us,' she remarked, 'But there are eight beds and seven are taken.'

'Oh, that'll be Elaine Wilson,' said Barbara knowledgably, 'she joined last term and is really a little old for the first form but as she didn't seem to have learned much at her previous schools, she's staying on in the first. She was here all summer as well you know,' she added, dropping her voice, 'Father and I went away for a couple of weeks, and she was still there when we came back.'

'Poor soul,' said Beryl gently, wrinkling her nose in distaste. 'Fancy her parents leaving her at school all hols.'

'I think they live abroad,' explained Barbara vaguely, then, looking at her watch, she added, 'Come on let's hurry up and unpack. We might just have time to have a look at the pool before tea.'

The pool was where the girls were allowed to swim in the warmer summer months. It was a perfect circle sunk into the ground surrounded by a few large shady trees and overlooking an expansive view of the surrounding woods and fields.

Having completed their unpacking the first formers trooped up to the pool which was situated on the front lawn close by to the houses, sheltered by a little copse of trees.

They were admiring the view and the inviting depths when a shrill persistent ringing broke the silence.

'That's the tea bell,' said Barbara unnecessarily, leading her little group of protégés back to the house, 'Goodness knows who rings it, they must have quite an arm on them.'

'We have breakfast and tea in our houses,' she continued as they skipped along, 'dinner we have in the hall.'

The dining room was large with lots of windows. Each form had their own table with the serving dishes placed in the middle. A member of staff sat at the head of each of the lower school tables.

On taking their seats the first formers saw that there was already a girl there. She, however, did not look up. The mistress at the head of the table shook her head sadly at the girl's lack of manners and gestured for the others to sit down.

She was a tall willowy looking person with a dreamy expression. Her hair was piled up on top of her head in an attempt at a bun and she had, Poppy noticed, as she took the seat next to her, enormous feet.

'Bonsoir, mes enfants,' she beamed in a surprisingly deep voice, 'I am your French teacher, Mademoiselle Meuhourat.'

'Mamzelle Mole Rat?' echoed Poppy, whose French was, as one previous mistress had once optimistically put it, 'Somewhat lacking.'

The whole table burst out laughing and even Elaine Wilson managed a smile.

Mamzelle rapped on the table with her spoon, annoyed, 'Ça suffit.' She turned to Poppy, who was still eyeing her, apparently completely at a loss to understand what she had said that was so funny. Mamzelle's anger vanished at the sight of the girl's angelic face, and she managed to convince herself, with an effort, that the girls were laughing, not at her name, but at Poppy's bad French. 'Ah, la pauvre fille. Girls, you must not laugh. My name is Mademoiselle Meuhourat.'

'Oh,' said Poppy, her brow clearing.

Of course, after this episode Mademoiselle Meuhourat was forever known as Mamzelle Mole Rat among the girls.

Porcine Pranks at St. Anne's

In the meantime, the table dissolved into excited chatter, with Barbara pointing out all the various mistresses.

'That's Miss Porter,' she said, indicating a mistress at the next table who was laughing and joking with the second formers. She had a head of short gingery brown curls and bright blue eyes. Nan thought she looked a jolly sort until she caught a glint in her eye as the mistress saw the girl watching her.

'She's a good sort,' said Barbara in a low voice, 'But she's awfully strict so don't go getting any ideas.'

'Who's that?' asked Nan, nodding towards a small, pink old lady with snowy white hair sticking out from a soft wrinkled face.

'That's Miss Whyte, the art and sewing mistress,' explained Barbara, 'She's a dear. And then there are other mistresses who eat at the other houses: Miss Knight; Mamzelle Leroy, the other French mistress and Miss Sparks. They're all good eggs.'

'How do you know all this?' asked Nan, teasingly.

Barbara gave her a sly look, 'Well you do pick up things living next door and I've had my spies in the past. Sometimes I've been asked to run errands....'

'So, you can't have been to school before then?' queried Poppy, reaching over to take what Nan could have sworn was her fourth bread roll.

'No, well I had my father and a tutor,' explained

Barbara, 'I've been waiting for so long to come to St Anne's. How about you?'

'I've worked on the farm up until now,' said Poppy, 'There was a school at the village, but I didn't spend much time there. Then mother began to get worried about my education and my aunt said she'd help to pay towards my coming to St Anne's, so here I am.'

'Don't your parents miss an extra pair of hands on the farm?' Barbara wanted to know.

Poppy gave a wry smile, 'To be honest I think they were glad to get rid of one of us. I've got four older brothers-'

'Good Lord, four!'

'-and three younger ones!' finished Poppy grimly.

For a moment Nan and Barbara could only stare at the girl, speechless. Then Barbara phewed a bit before turning to Nan, 'And what about you? Personally, I'm an only child, but do you have any siblings?'

'Just the one brother,' laughed Nan, 'Phil.'

'You sure? You haven't got six more stashed away somewhere?'

'No, just Phil. He's only a year younger than me so he'll be starting at St Becket's next year.'

'Really?' said Poppy. 'That will be nice.' Looking about their table at all the pairs of chattering girls, she suddenly became aware of Elaine Wilson staring at them. Thinking the girl looked a little lonely Poppy

Porcine Pranks at St. Anne's

attempted to include her in their conversation. 'Elaine, isn't it? We were just talking about our siblings. Do you have any brothers or sisters?'

A strangled sound halfway between a tut and a hiss burst from the girl and Poppy was shocked to be on the receiving end of a poisonous glare, before the girl rose sharply and fled from the room.

'Well!' exclaimed Poppy, astonished, 'Whatever's got into her? Fancy rushing off like that. Do you think I ought to go after her?'

Barbara raised a quizzical eyebrow, 'No Poppy. Let her be. She'll open up when she's ready. At the moment I think all you'd get would be a black eye.'

'Are you sure?' persisted Nan, 'she looked terribly upset.'

'Nan, Poppy, Elaine isn't some poor mite. Miss Porter made me swear not to tell you; she wanted her to have a fresh start. Let's just say the Second Form look awfully glad to be rid of her.' So saying she threw a glance over at the Second Form table who were indeed the picture of jollity, tucking into bread and jam, fruit and cake as if they hadn't had a meal all hols..

After tea the girls would normally spend an hour or so in the common room but on the first day they were judged to be practically falling asleep on their feet after their long journeys, so were packed straight off to bed.

Barbara, having only come a couple of hundred feet, looked put out at this and said as much to Matron.

Matron, however, was tired herself and wasn't going to stand for any of what she termed monkeying around.

'Off to bed with you,' she said sternly, adding coaxingly 'If you go now, you can have ten minutes reading time.'

This pacified Barbara who was soon between the sheets engrossed in a novel. Nan, whose bed was opposite, read the words on the cover; 'Something Fresh' by P. G. Wodehouse.

Barbara sensed her watching, and, replacing the bookmark as Matron reappeared, remarked, 'It's an awfully funny book. I've got one or two of his, I'll lend you one if you would like'

'Thanks,' replied Nan as Matron came waddling up the aisle between the beds, letting out an immense shhh which sounded like air escaping from a burst tyre.

'Lights out now girls,' she said, and suiting the action to the word, she disappeared.

A shaft of moonlight streamed through the curtains falling on Barbara's face as she lay opposite. Nan let out a contented little sigh. She felt she was going to like it at St Anne's, especially now that she had two friends.

Looking about the room, Nan caught sight of Zhang Wang Li in the bed next to Barbara's and frowned slightly. The girl puzzled her. She hadn't said a word yet but Nan had caught her staring at her several times which was a little unnerving. She can't be able to speak English, thought Nan, but then why would she be at an English school – it didn't make any sense.

However, Nan was far too tired to ponder on the problem any longer, and turning over, soon fell asleep.

Miss Porter, on peering into the First Form dormitory half an hour later was pleased to see a room full of soundly sleeping girls.

One girl, however, was not asleep but only pretending. Elaine Wilson had gone to bed early, not wishing to be disturbed by the others, but she lay awake, her mind churning, and it was a long time before she eventually fell asleep.

3

Wang Li's Story

When Nan awoke the next morning, she couldn't for the life of her think where she was. Then, still half asleep, she turned over and saw the seven other beds and the six sleeping girls and it all came back to her. She hugged herself happily; she was at St Anne's – what fun they were going to have!

Unable to remain in bed a moment longer, Nan drew back the bedclothes and slid her feet into the pair of slippers that sat on the floor waiting. Glancing at her alarum clock she saw that it was just coming up to seven o'clock; the dressing-bell would be going soon anyway.

Glad to have the bathroom to herself, Nan washed and dressed, appearing in the dormitory again just in time to see Barbara bounce out of bed.

'Hello,' exclaimed the girl, 'A fellow early riser.' The two of them sat on Barbara's bed chatting for a few minutes before the trilling of a bell signaled the awakening of the others.

The room was immediately filled with groans and creaks and thuds as girls jumped out of their beds. Poppy was up almost at once, terribly anxious that she had overslept. 'Goodness, I must have been tired. Why, on the farm, I get up at five.'

Beryl Forsyth, on the other hand, refused to move and seemed intent on spending the whole day in bed.

The others bustled about getting ready, the minutes ticking by, and still the girl didn't budge.

'Come on,' said Daisy May eventually, 'You really must get up old thing, or you'll be late for breakfast on your first day.'

'I know what'll get her up,' said Barbara, playfully brandishing a dripping wet sponge. Beryl jumped out of bed so fast that she went dizzy, and everyone laughed.

At last, everyone was ready and they trooped down to breakfast in the big dining hall. As toast, marmalade and porridge were devoured, Miss Porter went the rounds of the form tables, distributing time tables.

'French first thing,' remarked Poppy, 'Then Science, History and Latin, what a day!'

'Nothing with Miss Porter?' asked Beryl, trying to wrest the paper from Poppy's hands.

Wang Li's Story

'Hey, get your sticky paws off.'

'No, but we've got her all morning on Tuesday, look,' answered Barbara from the other side of the table.

Just then, Miss Porter herself appeared, and, commanding the first formers to follow her, proceeded to escort them up through the grounds to the schoolhouse.

It was a light crisp morning and the school seemed to glow in the pale sunlight. The grass underneath the girls' feet was dewy and the surrounding countryside, hazy in the slight mist that had formed, resembled a Georgian oil painting.

The crunch of gravel accompanied them to the grand double doors which were propped open. Inside, the entrance hall boasted a marble floor and stone columns. The first form mistress led them on up a carpeted staircase to their form room.

The first form classroom was a large room with windows down one side of it looking out towards the castle. There were four rows of desks split down the middle by the aisle. Altogether there was space for twenty four girls, although this term there would only be twenty three since Mamzelle Meuhourat's niece was unable to attend.

Meanwhile the first formers from Miss Sparks' House and Schoolhouse had turned up and were entering the fray for the cherished back row seats.

Zhang Wang Li secured the highly sought-after back

row window seat, Barbara Wofflespoon slipping into the seat next to her.

A cheeky looking girl from Miss Spark's House with a bob of red hair and dancing green eyes took the desk next to Barbara, winking as she did so. The two began chattering at once and appeared, as Poppy observed to Nan, 'as thick as thieves'.

Nan and Poppy managed to bag the two desks in front of Barbara and the Chinese girl and were joined by Beryl Forsyth. Daisy May seated herself across the aisle from Beryl and Elaine Wilson took the desk next to her but one. The empty seat between them remained that way despite being a third-row desk.

Finally, everyone had a desk and Miss Porter raised her voice to address her new form.

'Now that you have all found a place,' she began, her gaze sweeping round the class and lingering on the back row, 'We have half an hour to get to know each other,' taking a stack of paper from her desk, she continued, 'I'd like you all to write down your name and surname.'

Nan turned around in her chair, interested to see if Zhang Wang Li would understand these instructions.

Having looked around at the others, however, the Chinese girl appeared to understand very well what was required of her, for, bending over the paper she drew three beautiful characters:

Wang Li's Story

張望麗

Zhang Wang Li

Glancing across to the right, Nan noted that the impish girl with the red hair was called Leonora Jameson. She caught the Chinese girl staring at Leonora's red hair and realized that it was not just her that was new and unfamiliar to the girl. She had probably never set eyes on red or blond hair or darker skin before.

Just then, Miss Porter clapped her hands for silence and continued, her words making all the girls sit up and take notice.

'Now, I am sure you are all wondering who is to be Head Girl of the first form.'

Nan found herself looking at Elaine Wilson. Having already spent a term in Miss Porter's form, surely, she would be chosen as Head Girl. However, 'Miss Montagu and I have decided on...Daisy-May Brain.'

Daisy-May went red with pleasure as a cheer went up and those around her congratulated the girl.

Only one girl was displeased with this choice and that was Elaine Wilson. She hadn't ever really considered the matter but had taken it for granted that, as the oldest, she would be made Head Girl. It was only now that she realized how much she cared about it. Now she would have lost face with the others.

As a matter of fact, the decision had been a difficult one. 'Well Elaine Wilson or Barbara Wofflespoon would be the obvious choice,' Miss Montagu had said. 'I know that Elaine hasn't had the best of starts in your form, but this could be the making of her.'

'It could,' Miss Porter had agreed cautiously, 'Or the losing out of such a position of authority which she no doubt thinks is her due could be the making of her. Personally, I don't think she is ready for such a position of responsibility. As for Miss Wofflespoon, I don't believe we ought to further her ambitions. She would have too much of an advantage over the other girls.'

And so the two mistresses had consulted the various reports from the first formers' previous schools and had come up with Daisy May. And that girl was determined to show them that they had made the right decision.

Barbara, meanwhile, congratulated the girl heartily, quite unaware that she had even been in the running for the position.

Returning to the important tasks still to be done, Miss Porter ran through the list of classroom duties that the first formers would have to perform such as; topping up inkwells, changing the flowers that stood on the mistresses desk, tidying the classroom and fetching any new exercise books that were required from the big stationary cupboard in the corridor. The rota was pinned up on the noticeboard next to the large blackboard.

'Normally, of course, you would have an assembly during this time,' said the mistress, 'However there are still a few minutes left before Mamzelle is due to take you for French. Perhaps you could write your name and form on these books; it will save time tomorrow,' So saying, Miss Porter began distributing exercise books of three different pale pastel shades, Geography in green, Math's, red and English, pink. 'I said red for Math's Sarah,' she added sternly, her sharp eyes spotting the girl's mistake at once.

'Couldn't mine be pink?' she wailed, horrified for she was a girl who liked everything to be neat.

'You'll just have to put a line through it,' said the mistress shortly and moved on, leaving Sarah horror-stricken.

Nan wrote her own name, subject and form on each book before carefully blotting the wet ink. Lifting the lid of her desk she placed them in one corner. Then, taking her timetable from her pocket, she pinned it on the inside of the lid where she could easily see it when opening the desk.

'Mamzelle Meuhourat will be along in a minute,' said Miss Porter taking up a large pile of books, 'In the meantime, I expect you, Daisy May, to keep a reasonable amount of order.'

The first formers waited until they could no longer hear the mistress' shoes on the polished floor and then burst into excited chatter.

Porcine Pranks at St. Anne's

Daisy May manned the door, keeping an anxious lookout for Mamzelle. On seeing the mistress approach, she managed to quieten the others while she held the door open for the mistress.

Mamzelle Meuhourat was pleasantly surprised at such mature behavior from a class of first formers and beamed round appreciatively, 'Bonjour mes enfants. Today we will take a leetle test to see how well you understand the French, n'est-ce pas?'

'Ah, non, Mamzelle,' chorused the class.

'Mais oui,' stressed Mamzelle Meuhourat, proceeding to hand out papers, 'Ce n'est pas difficile. See I will even take it with you.'

The first formers bent over their test papers, a few grumbling and muttering darkly to themselves.

Nan found that the questions were really very easy, and it was only the last few that she struggled on.

To everyone's surprise, Zhang Wang Li showed herself to be top of the form in French. Mamzelle was delighted and so was the class when she embarked on an involved quizzing of the girl, quite forgetting to teach the others.

It transpired that Zhang Wang Li had had coaching in French and that her parents were in fact living in France. Mamzelle was quite beside herself when the girl said that they were living on the Franco Swiss border as Mamzelle herself was Swiss and came from that area.

Wang Li's Story

'Et avant ça vous habitiez en Chine, n'est-ce pas, ma chérie?' Excited to be able to talk to someone at last, Wang Li poured out her story. It sounded like something out of an adventure book to Nan and Poppy. Fleeing unrest in China, the Zhang family had sailed to Japan where they had spent three years before deciding to take the long ocean voyage west to Europe. Wang Li's father had a male cousin who had been sent to the trenches during the First World War and had stayed on in Europe making his life there. After having the services of a French tutor during the journey, the whole family could speak passable French. Having heard so much about the treasured English education, Wang Li's father, Zhang Chen had decided to send her to an English boarding school.

'Have you no siblings?' asked Mamzelle.

Wang Li explained that they had left her two grown up brothers in China caring for elderly relatives. Nan thought how hard it must be for the girl to be so far from her homeland and relations and what a huge shock the different culture must be to her. She wondered at her being sent to an English school when she was so obviously fluent in French whereas she appeared to understand very little English. But was that true? Sometimes when Nan looked at her she could have sworn that she understood every word. There was a mystery to be solved.

Porcine Pranks at St. Anne's

By the time Mamzelle had finished her conversation with Wang Li the lesson was at an end. She looked about her, startled, as the bell rung, before dismissing the class for break, still somewhat confused.

Nan was amazed to see the Chinese girl give a large wink to Leonora, who returned it, a broad grin on her face.

What had Nan just witnessed? Had Wang Li deliberately wasted the rest of the lesson by keeping Mamzelle Meuhourat talking? Definitely the girl was not at all as lost as she made out.

4

A Secret Shared

Poppy left the French lesson so hurriedly that Nan lost her and spent break with the others.

Poppy had sped off to the little box room to feed Bobby some things that she had smuggled off the breakfast table. She hid the piglet under her coat before taking her into the woods for a quick run around. Luckily Matron was busy in her little room, and nobody saw the two of them sneak back again.

Poppy was only just in time for their science lesson with Miss Sparks.

'Come in, come in,' said the mistress gruffly, 'Goodness, you look like you've run a marathon.'

Poppy was indeed very red in the face and more than a little breathless.

Porcine Pranks at St. Anne's

Miss Sparks was a stocky country person clad from head to toe in quietly fashionable tweeds with short windswept hair. She somehow gave the impression of being taller than she really was. Everyone gave her their full attention, even Leonora, and the lesson proceeded fluidly with many witty asides by the mistress which she confessed were to keep the girls from being bored not that there was much chance of that when all of Miss Sparks' favourite experiments involved explosions.

As the girls flooded out of the classroom for dinner Leonora remarked that she couldn't wait for their first practical lesson.

'I can't imagine Miss Sparks in a lab coat somehow,' said Nan.

'Well, you won't have to wait long. We're having a practical lesson on Friday,' said Barbara, joining them,' I just asked her.'

The dinner hall was brimming with girls and mistresses swarming about like bees. Indeed, the hum of noise that hit you on entering the hall was not unlike that which emanated from a beehive.

During lunch Barbara pointed out more mistresses but Nan and Poppy were intent on cramming as much food as they possibly could into the recesses of their clothing, whilst also attempting to consume as much as they could.

Barbara's sharp eyes took all of this in at once and she raised her eyebrows quizzically. Wang Li was also staring at the two of them and seemed to be on the verge of tears for trying not to laugh. The others noticed the lack of food in the two girls' vicinity and seemed to be hampering under the misapprehension that they had demolished it themselves.

'I say!' squealed Beryl, 'You two must be hungry. I don't know where in the world you put it because you're both so thin. How many cucumber sandwiches have you had, Poppy?'

Poppy stuffed a spoonful of treacle sponge into her mouth to avoid answering and then grabbed Nan by the wrist and pelted out of the hall.

Once they were outside, the two of them slowed down, Nan sensibly pointing out that they would get stomachache.

Once again Bobby was smuggled out for a walk in the woods and a meal of the things the girls had taken at dinner. As the break was longer this time, the two were able to relax a bit more and thoroughly enjoyed fussing over the little piglet – who, Poppy realized, wouldn't stay little for very long.

The other first formers, of course, were quite unable to imagine where the pair had been, and Nan began to feel that perhaps they ought to let the others in on the secret. It would certainly be good to have a few extra pairs of hands to help care for Bobby. Poppy, for her part, was also beginning to think that they had bitten off more than they could chew. It was certainly not her intention that Nan should put herself out for her – Poppy's –pet. Both girls secretly made up their minds to speak to the other about it that night.

After dinner the first formers had their first lesson with Miss Knight, who not only taught History, but also games. She had very long blond hair in a big swishy ponytail, and being a very patient and enthusiastic teacher, was a favourite with the girls.

Most of the first formers were hoping to make it onto the Lower School lacrosse team with the exception of Beryl Forsyth, Elaine Wilson and Sarah Mannering. As for Zhang Wang Li – well, she had never seen a lacrosse match before and shook with suppressed laughter to see the third formers practicing on the lower lawn.

Mamzelle Meuhourat, who happened to be passing, was most alarmed but readily accepted the explanation saying, 'Ah, yes, the English girls; to run about with the net on the stick – c'est vraiment fou, n'est-ce pas?'

The last lesson of the day was Latin with the Headmistress Miss Montagu. Miss Montagu was middle aged with a head of jet-black hair, neatly pinned up. Her face was strangely youthful, and her dark eyes shone with a light that seemed to take in everything.

Immensely placid, one got the impression that nothing could ever shock Miss Montagu, and whereas no one would ever dare to disobey Miss Porter or Miss Sparks, no one would ever think of disobeying Miss Montagu. She held the first formers captivated.

Nan, who had always thought Latin a very dry subject indeed was astonished to find that she had actually enjoyed it.

Miss Montagu somehow succeeded in bringing the extinct language to life – teaching the girls not only the complex vocabulary needed to follow the works of historians and chroniclers but also the everyday Latin that would have been used by everyone in the Roman Empire.

Only Poppy became occasionally lost in her own thoughts, gazing out of the window at the boarding houses and trying to imagine how her pet might be faring.

'Unde veniunt filii tui?' Miss Montagu asked suddenly, startling Poppy out of her meditations.

'Oh, er, sorry, what?' asked a red-faced Poppy.

'Unde veniunt filii tui?' repeated the headmistress patiently.

'Oh, erm,' Poppy glanced at her book and then at Nan, 'Filii mei ab Germania veniunt?'

'Very good,' said a pacified Miss Montagu, satisfied, 'I was afraid you'd gone to sleep there, but, no, very good.'

Porcine Pranks at St. Anne's

Poppy turned a deeper shade of red and concentrated on her Latin for the rest of the lesson.

Later, when the first formers were walking across to Miss Porter's House, Poppy sought Nan out and told her that she planned to let the others in on her secret. Nan felt immensely relieved and agreed readily.

'We'll all go into the woods at dinner break tomorrow, and I'll fetch Bobby,' said Poppy decisively, 'I'll tell the others in the common room tonight.'

The other first formers were most intrigued to discover what Poppy wished to show them and were in a state of acute excitement all the morning. They wolfed down their dinner so as to be at the woods as soon as possible.

Poppy dashed off to fetch Bobby and came back with her coat bulging. When they saw the tiny little piglet poking her face out of the girl's thick woolen coat, the first formers squealed in delight.

'Oh, isn't she cute!'

'Poppy, may I hold her?'

'I never knew a piglet could be so cute!'

'Do let me take her for a walk Poppy!'

Poppy beamed round at everyone, and Bobby was passed eagerly from one to the other of them. Nan felt a lot happier now that the other first formers were going to help look after Poppy's pet and keep her secret. And it was so much more fun to share the excitement with the others. Nobody noticed, however, that not all the first formers were there. Elaine Wilson was missing for she had not been in the common room when Poppy had made her announcement. Seeing the happy flushed faces of the others as they returned for afternoon lessons, Elaine felt puzzled, the others had a secret, she was sure of it, and they were not going to tell her.

Well, she was jolly well going to discover what it was and when she did, those jumped-up first formers were going to have to watch their step all right!

5

Nan Makes an Enemy

Throughout the first week the first formers took it in turns to care for Bobby. They had now realized that Elaine had been missed out and did not share the secret but somehow no one quite liked to tell her. She was always so short-tempered and seemed intent on keeping up her bad mood all term, so Elaine remained in the dark. Meanwhile the girls had met all their new teachers by now. There was Miss Whyte, the sewing and art mistress who seemed to wander around in a world of her own but was really very good at her crafts. Though she seemed to struggle to distinguish the girls faces at four feet away, she had surprisingly nimble fingers and produced some of the most intricate and charming embroidery the girls had ever seen. She invariably forgot their names, but nobody minded in the least, though it did present problems occasionally.

'Joan,' said Miss Whyte sternly one time, gazing distraitly over the top of her glasses, 'Where are the flowers I asked you to get for that blue vase?'

As no one in the first form went under the name of Joan, this criticism was met with silence.

'I'm surprised she can see that the flowers haven't been refreshed,' whispered Leonora to Barbara.

'I may not be able to see them, Lavinia, but I can smell them,' scolded Miss Whyte furiously.

Eventually, after a good deal of detective work, it was concluded that 'Joan' was Sarah of School House who had asked her friend to change the flowers for her and she had forgotten.

Miss Whyte grumbled about not getting other people to do one's own chores and sent Sarah rushing off to cut fresh flowers.

On a Wednesday morning the first formers had art with Miss White followed by drama with Miss Winter who also taught individual girls piano lessons. Beryl Forsyth and Zhang Wang Li were the only two first formers to take piano lessons and both reported that Miss Winter was 'terribly tiresome' and 'bad' respectively. Beryl very almost lost her temper and decided to give up on her lessons before she had really begun for she was a proud girl who never did anything she didn't want to. However, she did badly want to be able to play the piano so she stuck to it and instead turned on her charm, as Barbara put it, ingratiating herself with the mistress by doing any little thing she could to help.

Nan's first lesson with Miss Winter did not bode well for the rest of term. Miss Winter took an instant and virulent dislike to Nan which was quite illogical and could only be the result of racial prejudice. On seeing Nan, the drama mistress scowled and began to scold the girl for not tying back her hair. Now, Nan's hair was really quite short enough to be worn down as other girls with short hair did and though her Afro hair stuck out around her face it did not fall in her eyes and no other mistress had any concerns about it.

Miss Winter, however, was of the opinion that Nan's hair was 'too big' and that 'other pupils would not be able to see the board'.

Nan was momentarily stunned by the gross exaggeration of this perceived argument. She saw the amazed looks of her friends and felt somewhat mollified, but Miss Winter's unjust criticism had stung her, and she felt angry tears starting to her eyes. But then Poppy was taking her arm and leading her out of the classroom.

'Come on old girl,' she said in a low voice, 'we'll have to humour her. I'll put you in some plaits and

Nan Makes an Enemy

make sure that it takes an awfully long time and with any luck the lesson will be almost finished by the time we get back.'

Nan had introduced her friend to her special afro comb with its flat shape and elongated teeth and Poppy was, under careful guidance, becoming quite adept at using it. Nan was grateful for her friend's help, but she couldn't but feel that there would be more battles ahead with a person like Miss Winter.

Sure enough, on their return the drama mistress attempted to punish them for wasting lesson time. Luckily Beryl stepped in, the look of genuine disgust on her face frightening Miss Winter into dropping her charges.

All the first formers were glad when the bell rang for dinner and Nan and Poppy were the first out.

'I can't believe her,' fumed Beryl, 'she's so utterly disgusting!'

'Then why do you suck up to her so much?' demanded Leonora accusingly.

Beryl grimaced, 'It saves me a lot of pain,' she admitted, 'and it might prove useful someday. Besides there is something terribly satisfying about having someone like that in your debt and knowing that they have no idea how much you hate them.'

Everyone had to laugh at Beryl's peculiar logic.

'Well,' said Barbara, 'I suppose that's one way of

looking at it. Personally, I just want to waste the least amount of time on the woman. However, I also want to teach her a lesson. What say you, Leonora?'

The two girls exchanged a knowing look and Leonora allowed herself a smirk.

'I feel a trick coming on, 'she said softly, 'if there's one person who is positively asking for a trick to be played on her it's Miss Winter.'

'It's a jolly good thing we only have her once a week,' snapped Poppy who had been stewing quietly for over an hour, 'any more and I might just murder her. I'm only joking,' she added through gritted teeth as the others exchanged alarmed glances, 'she's not worth it.'

Nan squeezed her friend's hand; she was touched by the way her friends had come to her defence and she felt heartened. The only two people who hadn't uttered a word of sympathy were Elaine Wilson, who seemed completely wrapped up in her own gloomy thoughts as usual, and Wang Li who was sitting up very straight in her chair, a sort of look of frozen horror about her.

The Chinese girl still barely said a word in lessons, but she was becoming more and more talkative when the girls were alone in the common room and, of course, she was always very eager to converse with Mamzelle Meuhourat.

Nan Makes an Enemy

Nan threw herself into life at St. Anne's, spending most of her free time with Poppy on the Lacrosse field practicing catches.

Daisy-May would occasionally join them though she often kept Beryl company in the common room where she would be busy sewing or painting, or else out riding which was one of the girl's favourite pastimes.

Barbara and Leonora spent most of their time sitting in the common room or strolling round the grounds, heads close together plotting all kinds of tricks.

Wang Li had her piano lessons which she was finding more and more intolerable. It was clear that Nan was not the only person to be on the receiving end of Miss Winter's spite.

On top of her piano lessons, Wang Li spent a lot of time out on the top lawn practicing all kinds of intriguing postures, kicks and punches.

She laughed when Nan questioned her about it, 'Oh, I have to keep up my practice in gōng fū.'

'Gong fū,' repeated Barbara, 'what's that, some sort of martial art?'

Wang Li nodded.

'Do all your family train at it?' demanded Beryl, wide-eyed.

Wang Li grinned, 'No, not at all. Only me and Grandpa. He tried to teach my two older brothers, but they were never very interested, and my parents never

Porcine Pranks at St. Anne's

learnt. Whilst we were in Japan I also learnt some of their martial arts so I know mixture.'

'Well, I wish you'd teach me. I bet it's jolly useful,' interposed Leonora.

Wang Li narrowed her eyes, suspecting flippancy, 'First,' she instructed severely, 'Learn to touch your toes and to do the splits, then I can teach you.'

'Crikey!' exclaimed Leonora, 'I'm no gymnast. I can see I'll have to be more careful what I wish for.'

All the while the first formers were taking it in turns to smuggle Bobby out for walks and to feed her. The amount of food that she could consume was fast becoming terrifying and Poppy knew that she was growing - and growing quickly. How much longer she would be able to pick Bobby up and it would remain feasible to keep her in secret, she did not know.

Someone else who was worried about Bobby was Daisy-May who had been surprised and pleased to be made head of the form and wanted to be a success. The realities of the job with which she had been entrusted were, however, becoming clear to the girl. There were some very strong characters in the first form who, she knew, would be unwilling to accept authority from her. The problem of Bobby presented difficulties. Miss Porter would take a dim view of her aiding and abetting Poppy to keep her pet pig at the school. But she could not just turn the girl in; that would be cruel. Besides Poppy was her friend and the whole of the first formers in Miss Porter's house were also involved including herself. Perhaps she could induce Poppy to take Bobby to the stables so that she could be properly cared for there. But what if Bobby were to be sent home – that would be too awful. Poppy would never forgive her, and she would lose the trust and friendship of the whole form. Poppy herself might get in serious trouble and it would be all her fault, just for trying to help. Oh dear, what was she to do?

6

Trouble for the First Form

Whilst the others enjoyed their life at St. Anne's to the full, Elaine Wilson seemed to be sinking deeper and deeper into a gloomy depression. Initially the first formers had attempted to draw her out of this depression by suggesting games or walks or tying to engage her in conversation. However, after receiving only monosyllabic replies, usually in the negative this practice was abandoned. Elaine saw the others having fun, seemingly without a care in the world and, instead of trying to become one of them, began to despise them more and more. She still felt hurt not to have been chosen as head girl of the first form and jealous of the friendship of the others. She determined to wipe the smiles off their silly faces without seeing that this could bring no happiness to herself or anyone else.

It wasn't long before an opportunity presented itself for Elaine to wreak her spite on the unsuspecting first formers.

Skulking in the common room one breaktime, Elaine peeped out into the corridor to see Poppy returning from the daily outing to the woods, Bobby clutched in her arms, her blazer only partially hiding her.

Elaine let out an involuntary gasp, so great was her shock at this unexpected spectacle. So this was the others' secret. Pets at St Anne's were strictly forbidden unless housed at the stables with the school riding horses and provided with up-to-date health certificates. Miss Porter would have a fit if she knew about the first formers keeping a pig at school. Why, Poppy may even be expelled! Elaine smiled maliciously to herself at the thought.

Seeing the girl complete with pig disappearing downstairs to the little box room, Elaine followed cautiously. From the top of the stairs, she watched as Poppy seemed to vanish into thin air before reappearing pigless a moment later and skipping downstairs, whistling a carefree little tune.

Elaine followed where she had seen Poppy go and found the hidden staircase. The key to the box room was

Porcine Pranks at St. Anne's

in the lock so that, now that all the other first formers were in on the secret, they could all get in easily without needing to ask Poppy for it.

The key turned in the lock and Elaine saw the inside of the little room, and there was Bobby, curled up on a rug in the corner. The girl moved forwards to pick her up but Bobby, not recognizing this new smell, had other ideas and, neatly avoiding Elaine's outstretched hands, bolted for the open door.

Elaine straightened up, annoyed but felt better when she thought how dismayed the others would be when they found that their pet was missing. It would jolly well serve them right for not letting her in on the secret! The girl smiled smugly to herself all through afternoon lessons and her classmates were quite unable to account for the change in the normally sullen girl.

Bobby had other plans and, neatly avoiding Elaine's outstretched hands, bolted for the open door.

However, there was more trouble brewing for the first form. After prep. that night Miss Porter summoned Wang Li to the little study that she shared with Mamzelle Meuhourat.

Wang Li knocked with some trepidation and, on hearing the mistress' clear voice bid her enter, did so.

Miss Porter was standing behind her desk, a letter in her hand.

'Shut the door, please, Wang Li,' she said curtly, and the girl rushed to do as she was told before sitting down in the chair opposite the first form mistress.

'Did I say that you might sit down?' snapped Miss Porter and Wang Li sprang up again at once.

'I see that you understood that,' remarked the mistress smoothly, 'It may interest you to know, Wang Li, that I wrote to your parents expressing my concern at your limited understanding of the English language.'

Wang Li's eyes widened in horror at this unexpected news.

'I have here a reply from your mother saying she is quite at a loss to comprehend my concerns. Apparently you took classes in English during the three years you spent living in Japan and are more or less fluent,' went on Miss Porter, 'Well, what am I to reply? Pray tell me, am I to reiterate my concerns and bring this matter to the attention of Miss Montagu or am I to back down and express my apologies to your parents for the peculiar misunderstanding that appears to have arisen?'

All this was rapped out very quickly and would have been far too complex for the Wang Li of two minutes ago to understand. The new Wang Li, however, understood the mistress perfectly and felt the full force of her eloquence.

The Chinese girl was very much in awe of Miss Montagu and couldn't bear the thought of her knowing of her silly trick. There had been some concern at Wang Li taking Latin for it was thought to be far too much for her to take in. Wang Li, though, had a gift for learning languages and was one of the Latin mistress' star pupils.

Appalled by Miss Porter's threat, Wang Li could only croak, tears starting to her eyes.

'I am frankly astonished at your deceit I should have thought that you, of all people, would have seen the value of your education here and taken that chance with both hands,' scolded the first form mistress unsympathetically, 'I am disappointed in you.'

Wang Li gave a stifled sob quite unable to meet the mistress' eyes.

'Do I have your word that you will knuckle down and that there will be no more of this nonsense?' pressed Miss Porter mercilessly.

The girl nodded desperately, unable to speak.

'Thank you. I know that this move must be a very big change for you Wang Li, but you evidently have a gift for languages,' added the mistress unexpectedly, unbending a little, 'it would be a shame if you were to let that talent go to waste. You may go now.'

Wang Li went blindly out of the study and Leonora, who was passing with Nan and Barbara, was astonished to see the girl's red eyes and wet face.

'Hallo!' she exclaimed in a low voice, 'that can't be Wang Li? Why, I've never once seen her cry! I wonder what on Earth's the matter with her?'

Nan, noticing the door that her friend had come out of and thinking that it couldn't be long before the Chinese girl's secret was out, half guessed at the truth.

Whilst the others were dancing away to a gramophone record in the common room, Nan slipped out to find Wang Li and eventually tracked her down in the first form dormitory. She was lying on her bed, a faraway look in her eyes. As Nan entered, she sat up and gave the girl a watery smile.

'Are you all right?' asked Nan tentatively.

'I'm fine,' lied Wang Li, shaking back her long, straight hair and giving Nan an encouraging grin. Nan smiled back, thinking how like the irrepressible Leonora the girl looked.

'Miss Porter found me out and I suppose she was pretty sore about it. I was planning to take another few days to master the English language, but I shall just have to surprise everyone with my quick learning.'

'Nan,' continued Wang Li in serious tones, getting up from the bed and taking her friend's hands in hers, 'I owe you an apology. I thought you were in some way different from me. At school in China, I was always taught that the Han Chinese were superior to other races. I'd never known anyone like you before, but I see now how wrong I was; I should have known better. Please accept my humblest apology.' Wang Li bowed her head and Nan felt slightly silly at such ceremony though she knew it was normal in China. Looking into the girl's anxious eyes, she knew that she was sincere.

'I accept your apology; of course, I do. I don't suppose you knew any better,' said Nan thinking how much damage ignorance could do in this world.

'But you did,' blurted out Wang Li urgently, 'Well, I mean, I don't suppose there are that many people who look like me around here. Had you ever seen anyone like me before?'

Nan smiled, 'Only at the picture palaces,' she admitted, 'But I think it's different for you. Chinese is such a different language from English that it must feel quite cut off from the rest of the world.'

'I'll teach you Mandarin Chinese!' volunteered Wang Li readily and then laughed as she saw Nan's doubtful expression. 'Ni hao- that's hello'

'Knee how,' repeated Nan shyly and Wang Li nodded. 'Bù cuò- not bad.'

Porcine Pranks at St. Anne's

Nan shook her head modestly, 'I'll never be able to learn as many languages as you, Wang Li.'

'I don't see why you shouldn't,' objected Wang Li, 'You're excellent at French.'

'Well, give me a phrase every now and then and we'll see,' said Nan and the Chinese girl beamed.

A silence fell between the two of them before Wang Li broke it by saying abruptly, 'I'm sorry Nan, but may I just feel your hair?'

For some reason this made Nan feel a little embarrassed but she realised that the Chinese girl was simply curious and meant no harm so she said, 'All right but only if I can feel yours as well.'

'Of course,' replied Wang Li, putting out a hand to Nan's thick frizzy hair. Nan felt the Chinese girl's soft straight hair between her fingers.

It was just at this moment that Barbara burst through the door to stop short, surprised at the scene of the two girls solemnly feeling each other's hair that met her eyes, 'Hello, hello, hello,' she exclaimed, laughingly, 'What have we here?' Then without waiting for an answer she continued in a serious voice, 'I say, Nan, Wang Li, the most awful thing's happened! Poppy went up to the box room just now to see Bobby and the door was wide open and Bobby gone! Poor Poppy's most terribly upset.'

The three girls exchanged alarmed glances before racing from the room. Poppy was sitting in an armchair,

Nan felt the Chinese girl's soft, straight hair between her fingers.

Porcine Pranks at St. Anne's

her knees up under her chin, blowing her nose loudly on her pocket handkerchief.

'Oh, poor Bobby!' she cried thickly, 'it's all my fault!'

Beryl came in just then, a book under her arm, and was told the news, 'You idiot Poppy,' she said lightly, 'Fancy leaving the door open!'

'Don't be an ass, Beryl,' retorted Poppy hotly, 'As if I'd do a fool thing like that.'

'Well, you were the last one in there,' pointed out Beryl mildly.

'So I was,' said Poppy slowly, 'but I locked the door.'

'But you left the key in the lock, didn't you?' reasoned Nan, 'which means that anyone could have let Bobby out.'

'Oh, but who would do such a thing!' wailed Poppy.

There was a silence.

'I can think of someone,' stated Barbara grimly, 'Has anyone seen Elaine recently?'

'What are you getting at?' frowned Beryl, confused.

'Well, she's been looking jolly pleased with herself lately over something,' said Barbara still in the same grim voice, 'like the cat that's got the cream. I bet you anything she's behind this. I vote we tackle her about it tonight.'

'Wait,' interposed Daisy-May and, as head girl, everyone looked to her to hear what she had to say, 'it may have been an accident. It's possible someone else unlocked the door and Bobby took the chance to escape. One of the maids may have decided to go in there.'

Beryl snorted, 'No maid ever goes in there-'

She was quelled by a mock stern look from Barbara, 'This is our head girl speaking Beryl,' she said shocked, 'A little more respect, please. Yes Daisy- May, you were saying...'

'Thank you, Barbara,' said Daisy-May, trying not to smile, 'Well, I think we ought not to come to any sudden conclusions. I vote we wait until morning to come to a decision.'

As it happened there was no question of waiting until the morning because Bobby turned up that very evening as the first formers were getting ready for bed. She must have been able to smell her mistress' scent for she was right there curled up under Poppy's bed.

The girl gave a gasp of delight and pointed her out to Nan who was pulling on her pyjamas on the next bed, 'Why, she was under the bed the whole time!' she exclaimed joyfully.

Barbara, who had witnessed the little scene, put a warning finger to her lips and Poppy understood. Elaine Wilson was not far away; if she had had anything to do with Bobby's release, she might yet try to cause more trouble by splitting to Matron or Miss Porter.

Once the girl had entered the bathroom, Poppy

Porcine Pranks at St. Anne's

turned to Barbara, saying urgently, 'I must get her back to the box room quickly!'

Barbara, however, laid a staying hand on Poppy's shoulder, 'There's no time for that old girl, Matron will be along in a minute. You'll just have to shove her under the sheets and pray that she doesn't give the game away, or you'll be for it.'

Poppy was a little reluctant to do this for it seemed a reckless thing to do. She needn't have worried, however, for, hugging the piglet close to her, the sheets and blankets pulled up around her chin, neither Matron nor Elaine suspected a thing. Bobby was thoroughly well-behaved, giving only the occasional barely audible grunt of contentment. Poppy, once Matron had gone and she could relax, smiled widely under the cover of darkness, overjoyed to have an opportunity to spend the night with her beloved pet. She slept soundly, safe in the knowledge that the little alarum clock under her pillow would wake her in good time to return Bobby to the box room before the dressing bell would sound. And this time she would jolly well make sure that she pocketed the key!

Two people, though, had a far more disturbed night. One was Elaine, who never slept well. Tonight, she was plagued by a nagging doubt. She had seen how upset Poppy was at losing her pet, how she had cried and hardly had a bite to eat at tea. For the first time, Elaine began to feel something approaching regret regarding her actions. Then she remembered that the others could have let her in on the secret, but they had chosen not to. Whatever Poppy was suffering now she had brought on herself by being so mean to her, Elaine. Anyway, she hadn't meant to lose Bobby; she would have returned her after a couple of days. It wasn't her fault that the piglet had shot out of the door like that.

Reassured, Elaine drifted off into a fitful sleep.

The second person having difficulty falling asleep was Wang Li. Although she had pretended otherwise to Nan, Miss Porter's words had struck a chord within her. She felt very small and mean indeed when she thought how she had been deceiving people just to get out of doing so much work. She had so much more than her contemporaries living in a China racked with civil war, in fear off their lives, their futures uncertain. She had her freedom and security and a chance at a wonderful education if only she took it. And she had thought it a great joke to pretend to understand less English than she did in order to get out of working as hard. She had thought it funny. Wang Li determined to herself that she would work- from now on she would work hard. She couldn't promise not to indulge in the occasional joke or trick for she was a fun-loving girl, but these would be rare indeed. Oh, yes, St Anne's was about to see another side of Zhang Wang Li!

7

A Plague on Miss Winter

The mistresses of St. Anne's were most surprised and pleased by the sudden alteration for the better in Wang Li's understanding of the English language.

Miss Knight found that the girl now grasped her meaning when she tried to correct her technique at Lacrosse and, although Wang Li still believed the game a hilarious invention, she did improve. The girl's favourite lessons, however, were when they would go into the gymnasium with its highly polished wooden floor, its climbing bars up the walls, its benches and horses and its thick coloured mats. Wang Li could climb like a monkey and turn cartwheels without even placing her hands down. Barbara was also very supple and Leonora quite fearless, but Nan and Poppy and the others preferred their feet on solid ground, as Poppy put it.

Miss Sparks also noticed the change in Wang Li, causing her to exclaim, proudly, 'Good Lord, I think you've cracked it!' and starting the girls off on a round of applause. Wang Li had the grace to blush, and Nan also felt quite uncomfortable for her.

Miss Whyte, on being told the news by an excited Beryl, fluttered a bit, before saying, 'I'm as chuffed as a butty for you, duckie.' Which was a new one to Wang Li and actually had to be translated.

Miss Porter saw with pleasure the girl's increased effort and was, unbeknownst to Wang Li, immensely proud of her. Maths was perhaps the subject the girl struggled at the most and had before happily avoided the more complex sums and equations. Now, she tried to understand and, when her form mistress bade her come up to the blackboard and handed her the chalk, she was able to fill in half the sums written there.

Not everyone in the first form, however, was as determined to work hard as Wang Li. Elaine Wilson's work was consistently below the standard expected of her which meant she amassed a large amount of it to be redone. Barbara and Leonora, on the other hand, were consistently at the top of the class in most subjects despite Leonora putting in very little effort and constantly distracting her friend during lessons.

It happened that Leonora had recently received a package in the post from her male cousin, (who also attended boarding school and was also an imp). It contained numerous magazines devoted to the instruction of many imaginative tricks and it also contained what appeared at first glance to be a cardboard box of quite ordinary sticks of white chalk. Though identical in shape and size, texture and look, this chalk did not write.

Nan found the two friends on a bench in the high red bricked kitchen garden, planning in excited whispers.

'Hello,' she said, sitting down next to them, 'What are you two up to?'

'We think it's time we played some tricks on Miss Winter,' revealed Leonora in a low voice, a wicked grin splitting her freckled face.

'Yes,' agreed Barbara, her eyes sparkling, 'But she cannot suspect us- or indeed any particular class. Listen, this is what we'll do...'

Later that day, Miss Winter was alone in her large ground floor classroom marking work, as Barbara had ascertained she would be, when the window near her desk suddenly opened of its own accord. Miss Winter had a peculiar horror of open windows or fresh air of any kind and it was a chilly September day.

A Plague on Miss Winter

She went to the window, accordingly, pulling one of her assorted scarves closer around her neck, and shut it firmly.

No sooner had she returned to her desk than the temperamental window flew open again.

Frowning, the mistress crossed the room and tentatively stuck her head out, but there was no one in sight. Pushing the sash down decisively, she returned once more to her marking. This time fully five minutes went by before the window took on a mind of its own and shot up again.

Frustrated, Miss Winter leapt to the window determined to catch whoever it was. But the gravel drive, onto which the window faced was deserted.

Around the corner, however, two first formers, clinging to a thin length of so-called invisible string, were clapping hands over their mouths to stop themselves from laughing.

Suddenly a figure came striding up the path that led down to the boarding houses. It was Miss Sparks, looking brisk and slightly windswept.

At the sight of the science mistress, the two girls fled, their feet scrunching in the gravel. Miss Winter, also catching sight of her colleague, beckoned her over imperiously.

'Did you see who that was?' she demanded angrily.

Miss Sparks raised her eyebrows and thought

Porcine Pranks at St. Anne's

quickly; she had seen clearly enough that it was Wofflespoon and Jameson, but she hesitated to tell the drama mistress so. Miss Winter was a new mistress and had been engaged in somewhat of a rush after the old drama mistress had left unexpectedly to have children. Miss Winter had arrived with excellent references, but Miss Sparks did not like her. She found her bad tempered, ill-mannered and impatient- not qualities that were exactly endearing.

She showed her impatience now, urging, 'Well?'

'I'm afraid to say I didn't,' answered Miss Sparks untruthfully, 'I didn't have my glasses on you see,' she couldn't resist adding. Miss Winter accepted this excuse readily and the science mistress moved on her way, a slight smile twitching the corners of her lips. If Miss Winter had thought about that last remark of hers, she would have realised that Miss Sparks had indeed seen the troublemakers, for she was long-sighted, only wearing glasses for close-to work like reading.

Over the next few days, Miss Winter was plagued by a series of incidents- too small to be thought of as tricks but which she regarded with the greatest suspicion. Piles of books to be marked would go missing, only to turn up in the most unlikely places. Scripts would get mixed up and have to be sorted through once more. And then there was the box of chalk.

A Plague on Miss Winter

The drama mistress was teaching the third form and wanted to write down the main structural elements of the play that they were studying. She selected a stick of chalk from the shelf at the bottom of the blackboard and attempted to do so. Nothing happened; the chalk stolidly refused to make any mark at all.

Enraged, the mistress gritted her teeth and selected another likely looking candidate. It too refused to do it's job.

The third formers were all staring blankly at her. They certainly didn't look like they were behind any trick; besides Miss Winter liked the third form.

In the end, the mistress had to resort to dictating her ideas for the third form to write down in their notebooks, a proceeding that took an awful lot of repeating and spelling out of difficult words and consequently wasted lesson time.

Of course, Miss Winter could have sent one of the girls to borrow chalk from one of the other mistresses but somehow the drama teacher didn't want any of her colleagues to suspect that she was the victim of such pranks. Being new, she was afraid the others would think her incapable of keeping discipline.

The first formers were pleased with the success of their tricks. They really seemed to have got amongst the mistress, rendering her thoughtful and inattentive in lessons which was the way they liked her. Nan was particularly grateful for this change in the mistress as she had suffered the most at the drama teacher's hands and was now able to survive lessons almost unnoticed.

Everyone agreed that it was too dangerous to play an open trick during a lesson on Miss Winter as she was notoriously biased and likely to take the opportunity to punish Nan or Wang Li proof or no proof and no one wanted to risk that.

Leonora, however, was simply longing to play a trick on someone and she found her gloriously unsuspecting victim in Mamzelle Meuhourat.

The girl racked her brains for an idea involving Bobby the pig, for, although she had not yet broached the subject with Poppy, she was determined not to let such a brilliant opportunity pass. After all it wasn't every day that you had a clandestine pig stashed away to be brought out at a moment's notice. The comic value was infinite. She could sadly think of nothing.

Inspiration came one day as she and Barbara were on their way to a history lesson. They were taking the scenic route down the carpeted corridor off which the mistresses had their studies and bedrooms for those who slept in School House. The door to Miss Porter and Mamzelle Meuhourat's study was slightly ajar and Mamzelle's deep voice came sailing through it. She was holding a letter from her sister in Switzerland and reading passages aloud before translating them for the benefit of Miss Porter who had her head bent over some marking and did not appear to appreciate this solicitude.

'Ah, my sister, she suffers terribly,' wailed Mamzelle theatrically, 'Her heart it goes pitter pat, pitter pat, c'est tellement épouvantable ce qu'elle subit! She has the- what is the word- the halloocinasions!'

Leonora imagined Miss Porter's eyebrows soaring as there was a pause before she replied, 'Ah, you mean palpitations, Mamzelle. Yes, well, she has my sympathies but perhaps you could finish your letter in your head; I promised the Lower Sixth I'd mark their fieldwork essays for tomorrow.'

'In my head?' Mamzelle appeared quite uncomprehending.

'I mean to yourself. Look-' despairingly, 'If you must read aloud, I'm sure Mamzelle Leroy would be delighted to hear your sister's news.'

'Mamzelle Leroy? Ah, non, je ne sais pas,' Mamzelle Meuhourat sounded far from convinced. The two first formers carried on their way just as the door opened wide and the French mistress came out, letter in hand.

'Well,' breathed Leonora, her eyes alight with fun as the two friends rounded a corner, 'Mamzelle has just furnished me with the most marvelous idea for a trick.

Her sister may not suffer from hallucinations, but she is about to.' And very quickly, Leonora whispered her plan into Barbara's eager ear.

The girl stared at her friend admiringly, 'But Leonora,' she said worriedly, 'surely not even Mamzelle Mole Rat would fall for that.'

'She'll fall for it all right,' opined Leonora confidently as the two of them reached the door of their form room, 'Don't you worry about that!'

8

Bobby Joins the French class

That evening the first formers gathered in the Common room to hear Leonora's plan. One person however was missing and that was Elaine Wilson. The girl had gone down with a sore throat that afternoon and been packed off by matron to spend the night in the san.. Although she didn't want to wish a sore throat on anyone, Leonora couldn't help feeling glad that the girl was out of the way for she would otherwise have had to have been let in on the trick and indeed on Bobby's existence, for of course, no one knew that Elaine had found out about Bobby.

Leonora explained her plan quickly and concisely to the expectant first formers, who erupted into excited exclamations and questions. 'Oh Poppy', implored Leonora, 'do, do let us use Bobby in this trick. It'll be simply hilarious.' And the girl fixed Poppy with a pleading expression. The other first formers turned to stare beseechingly at Poppy and the girl had little choice but to give in. Nan, who was watching Leonora closely, saw the smirk of satisfaction flash across her face and realized that the girl had asked her friend with an audience of the other first formers deliberately. Why, of all the cheek! Still, Nan thought, it did sound a wonderful trick. Of course, it was a risk, for even if Mamzelle Meuhourat was taken in, another mistress would not be and Poppy's secret would be out. Perhaps, though, thought Nan, that was not a bad thing. After all, Poppy could not possibly keep Bobby hidden away forever.

'When will we play it, Leonora?' asked Beryl, clapping her small dainty hands and hopping up and down in her excitement. Leonora grinned, 'Well, it's Friday today. We have Mamzelle Meuhourat again on Monday. I suggest we play it then.'

'Oh yes! How marvelous. I can hardly wait!'

Wang Li found herself rejoicing at this welcome highlight in the monotony of schoolwork. As already mentioned, the girl was very fond of jokes and tricks. She may have promised Miss Porter to study hard at her lessons but that did not mean she could not enjoy Leonora's tricks.

'Someone will have to alert the first form girls from Miss Sparks' and School House so that they can play up to Mamzelle. Of course, I'll tell the other girls in Miss Sparks',' said Leonora quickly for she was not supposed to be in the first form common room of Miss Porter's House at all but had made a burglarious entry by way of a ladder that the gardener had left propped up by the shed. This was a very strict rule but one which Leonora frequently broke in order to spend time with Barbara. As Flora of Miss Sparks' put it, 'Leonora spends more time over at Miss Porter's than she does here.'

'I'll tell the School House girls,' volunteered Beryl. 'I get on with Sarah, so I'll tell her to pass the message on to the others.'

'Good. That's that sorted', said Leonora happily.

The first form girls were giddy with excitement that weekend. And Nan had another reason to be happy on the Sunday. She was walking next to Poppy with the other girls on the way to church when two sixth form girls came up alongside them. Both belonged to Miss Sparks' House and Nan had only ever seen them at dinner in the hall, but Barbara had pointed them out as the head girl and games captain.

The games captain, Amrita Kaur Anand was one of the few girls at St. Anne's who were not white British. She was of Indian origin with skin just a shade lighter than Nan's and a long thin plait of hair which she wore wound round her head when out on the Lacrosse field.

Porcine Pranks at St. Anne's

She also wore, Nan noticed, a thin silver band around her wrist, which the girl thought odd as girls were not allowed jewelry at St. Anne's and anyway Amrita was not the sort of girl to wear jewelry.

'Hello,' called the sixth former, 'you're Nan Miller, aren't you?' Nan nodded, too pleased to speak. 'I saw you practicing on the Lacrosse field yesterday. Keep going like that and you may make the team yet. We could do with another reserve!' So-saying Amrita clapped Nan jovially on the back and skipped off. The Head girl, Isobel Harding, a jolly red-faced girl with a twinkle in her eye, gave Nan a broad grin and a wave before following her friend into church. Nan stared after them, hardly able to believe her ears.

'I say', exclaimed Poppy heartily, 'Fancy Amrita noticing your lacrosse skills. You must be good.'

Nan blushed and took her friend's arm in hers, her head in a whirl.

French with Mamzelle Meuhourat was first thing on a Monday morning. Leonora and Poppy wolfed down their breakfast so as to have time to take Bobby out of the box room and hide her in a little disused shed in the vegetable garden. They then had to hurry back for assembly before returning quickly to transfer Bobby to a large walk-in wardrobe sort of thing, which was located very handily at the back of the first form

Bobby Joins the French class

classroom. What purpose it was supposed to serve no one knew but it served Leonora's purpose very well. Of course, all this required a good deal of concealment and creeping about to avoid being spotted. Poppy carried Bobby, covering her with her blazer, and found that it was getting really very difficult to conceal her. The piglet also appeared to be gaining a considerable amount of weight and thinking back to how tiny she had been as a newborn, Poppy estimated that she had more than doubled in size.

However, they made it at last and Bobby was safely installed in the glorified cupboard, with a bowl of potato peelings begged off the kitchen staff by Beryl, to keep her happy until the time when Mamzelle entered.

Mamzelle Meuhourat had had a day out on the Sunday with the French master of St. Becket's towards whom she held the warmest feelings. To think that he had chosen her over Mamzelle Leroy was a very pleasant thought indeed to Mamzelle Meuhourat and she was consequently in the best of moods.

'Bonjour mes enfants,' she said gaily. 'Merci bien ma chère Beryl,' she added, for Beryl had held the door open for the mistress.

'Today we continue with our dictée, n'est-ce pas? Open your books please and I will begin.'

The first formers all opened their desk lids to take out their books, a few of them grumbling as they did so.

Porcine Pranks at St. Anne's

For perhaps five minutes the lesson proceeded smoothly, then Barbara put up her hand to ask the meaning of a suitably long and difficult word. Mamzelle turned her back on the girls to write down the spelling of the word on the blackboard, its definition and any synonyms as she always did with a new word.

Quick as a flash Leonora was out of her chair and at the door of the cupboard. She handed Bobby to Barbara who deposited her unceremoniously in Leonora's chair and Leonora herself disappeared within the cupboard, leaving the door slightly ajar.

Mamzelle turned back to her class still explaining. The words died on her lips as her gaze fell on Bobby who had put her front trotters up on the desk and was snuffling Leonora's French book appreciatively.

'Tiens!' cried Mamzelle, a large hand flying to her heart. 'What is that animal doing here? And where is Leonora?'

The mischievous first formers exchanged puzzled glances.

'What animal Mamzelle?'

'Why whatever do you mean Mamzelle, Leonora's not moved'.

'Are you telling me that Leonora – she is in her chair still. Ah non, ce n'est pas vrai ça!'

'I'm right here Mamzelle,' came Leonora's voice, only slightly muffled.

Bobby Joins the French class

Mamzelle jumped a couple of feet in the air and clutched her heart again.

'Leonora is that you chérie?' she asked tentatively.

'Why, Mamzelle, whatever do you mean, of course it's me, said Leonora sounding exasperated.

'Mamzelle,' said Beryl, a worried expression on her face. 'Are you sure you're feeling all right? You don't have a temperature, do you?'

'Well, I do feel a leetle hot', admitted Mamzelle, 'but I am quite well'.

'You don't suffer from hallucinations do you Mamzelle?' asked Agnes seriously and Zhang Wang Li had to lift the lid of her desk to hide her mirth from the French mistress.

'From halloocinasions?' echoed Mamzelle. 'What is this word? I do not know him'.

'Well it's...,' began Agnes.

'Seeing things which aren't really there,' finished Millicent, a grave expression on her face, which was too much for Sarah who stuffed a handkerchief into her mouth to try to stop herself from laughing out loud.

While Agnes had distracted Mamzelle Meuhourat, Leonora had slipped back into her seat, exchanging places with Bobby. When the French mistress turned back, she got the shock of her life to see Leonora calmly sitting at her desk.

'Mon Dieu, Leonora you are returned.'

'Returned Mamzelle?' frowned Leonora with such a straight face that Poppy let out a snort of laughter which she quickly stifled into a hacking cough. 'Whatever do you mean? I've been here all the time'.

'But', began Mamzelle in consternation, then gave up, took a deep breath and said 'Ah well, what does it matter, you are here now, n'est-ce pas? Now, let us continue'.

So-saying, Mamzelle Meuhourat picked up her book and began reading from it again. Leonora was not going to let her get away with it that easily, however.

As soon as Beryl had got Mamzelle's attention and was asking her something, Leonora was out of her seat and Barbara was dropping the bemused piglet back into the girl's chair.

Straightening up, Mamzelle caught sight of Bobby once more at Leonora's desk and let out a shrill scream.

'Nom d'un nom d'un nom...' she exclaimed loudly and looked so shaken Daisy-May was afraid she might faint. The situation was now getting a little out of hand, with only a handful of girls still attempting to keep a straight face. Nan was shaking with laughter, tears streaming down her cheeks. Wang Li was laughing unrestrainedly. Sarah was valiantly trying to find space for a fourth handkerchief in her mouth and Beryl presently fell out of her chair for laughing.

Mamzelle Meuhourat, however, did not appear to

« Nom d'un nom d'un nom... »
She exclaimed loudly

'Mamzelle,' she said trying to sound as calm as possible, 'what is a pig doing in your classroom?'

'Ah non, that it is Leonora Jameson,' cried Mamzelle in distressed tones.

Miss Sparks' eyebrows came clean off her forehead and disappeared into her hair.

'Leonora Jameson?' she echoed faintly, then trying to keep her voice steady she added, 'Mamzelle, as a biology teacher I can assure you that I am one hundred per cent sure that that is a pig. What it is doing there and how it came to be there I could not say. Leonora Jameson, I've no doubt will be able to fill you in.' At these words, as if by magic, the cupboard door opened, and Leonora slunk out.

'Ah speak of the devil', said Miss Sparks, a hard note in her voice. 'Well, I'll leave you to it. I have a class of second formers with lit Bunsen burners to return to. Pip, pip'.

The mistress disappeared and Mamzelle Meuhourat bore down on Leonora, her eyes glinting wrathfully.

'Ah, méchante fille, you are a wicked girl, Leonora, n'est-ce pas? You deceive your poor old Mamzelle into believing she has the halloocinasions. My heart, he goes pitter pat, pitter pat, tu fais vraiment des bêtises, hein?'

'Yes Mamzelle,' said Leonora miserably.

'Tais-toi!' exploded Mamzelle, then suddenly the most curious noises erupted from the French mistress

Bobby Joins the French class

and the first formers saw to their astonishment that she was laughing.

Wiping a tear from her eye, Mamzelle sat down heavily behind the desk and attempted to calm herself. 'Ah', she sobbed, 'your face, ma petite! Your old Mamzelle plays a trick on you. Eh, bien, we must be quiet now mes enfants, or Mamzelle Sparks, she will return. We will settle down and continue with our dictée, yes?'

'Oh, Mamzelle,' said Leonora, her faced swathed in smiles once again; 'you are a sport'.

'Yes, a real brick!' added Beryl. Mamzelle looked puzzled but pleased. Ah these English girls she thought, they may trick their poor Mamzelle, but they were good at heart.

9

Miss Winter is a Nuisance

To the first formers' immense surprise they were to hear nothing more of their trick for a while. Mamzelle let Poppy out of the classroom with Bobby in her arms and Miss Sparks appeared to have put the incident clean out of her mind or perhaps she was hampering under the misapprehension that Mamzelle had dealt with it.

Bobby spent the night in the little box room again and Poppy and Leonora went to bed fondly imagining themselves to have got away with it.

The next morning, following assembly, Nan and Poppy were dawdling down a corridor, enthusing about the previous morning's trick, when a door was flung open, and Miss Winter peered out at them suspiciously.

Her eyes narrowed when she saw Nan and the girl stopped dead, suddenly cold.

'Nan Miller,' barked the drama teacher, 'Why is your hair not tied back? Do it at once!'

'But-' began Poppy in Nan's defence at the same time as Nan also opened her mouth to argue.

'Silence!' snarled Miss Winter looking half mad, 'you will write out 'I must make myself presentable' 100 times! To be handed in first thing tomorrow! Now be quick!' and with that the mistress shot back into the doorway from whence she had come, slamming the door behind her.

Poppy stuck out her tongue at the door but Nan could not smile, 'Hateful, hateful woman,' she fumed, her fists clenched so tightly the nails dug into her palms, 'If she thinks I'm going to write that so much as once, she can think again. And we haven't time to waste doing hair; we must hurry, or we'll be late for Miss Porter's lesson! Oh, blow!' Nan looked distraught. She blinked back tears and faced her friend. She had spoken bravely but she knew that she wouldn't really dare to disobey any mistress.

'We're already late,' said Poppy slowly, 'but, whatever else she is, Miss Winter is a St. Anne's mistress; we have to do as she says,' she added, a strange note in her voice.

Nan's shoulders slumped and her face fell, were they really powerless against Miss Winter?

Porcine Pranks at St. Anne's

'Come on,' said Poppy, the same mysterious note in her voice, 'I've got an idea!'

Twenty minutes later, Nan and Poppy stood outside the first form classroom. Nan could hear her knees knocking and Poppy's face was taut. Nan just hoped her friend's plan worked.

'You knock,' she whispered, 'It was your idea.'

'No, you knock,' rejoined Poppy, squirming.

'All right,' agreed Nan in a low voice. So, her heart pounding, she raised a fist and knocked tentatively.

'Enter!' came the first form mistress' voice and the two girls did so reluctantly. The storm broke.

'Well, where on Earth do you think you have been, the two of you? That's twenty-five minutes of lesson time that you will be catching up at break. Twenty-five! I have never known anyone turn up so late before. You had better have a very good explanation for this?' Then, as the two continued to stare in mute horror, 'Well, we are all waiting?'

'Miss Porter,' gasped out Nan, finding her voice at last, 'I- We- Miss Winter told me to do my hair and-'

The first form mistress frowned, then she took in Nan's neatly plaited hair, 'So, this is why you always do you hair so carefully on a Wednesday,' she said at last in a level voice. 'But Nan, I don't understand what Miss Winter should find wrong with your hair. Why should you have to spend so much time on it when it's perfectly short and nice as it is?'

This was so exactly what Nan thought herself that she could have no answer. The truth was, of cause, that Miss Winter saw nothing the matter with Nan's hair but made her do it up every lesson as a way of making difficulties and spiting her. Why did Nan feel so embarrassed all of a sudden? It wasn't her fault and she had done nothing wrong and yet she felt ashamed to have the whole class staring at her.

This solution to the matter seemed to strike Miss Porter, for, just as Poppy opened her mouth to try and explain the war the drama mistress had waged on Nan and Wang Li, she held up a hand to stop her, 'I think I see what's been going on here,' she said in a carefully controlled voice, 'I am not in the habit of allowing other mistresses to dictate my lesson time. I shall be speaking to Miss Winter about this. Nan rest assured that this will not happen again. Very well, you may take your seats, both of you.'

Nan and Poppy sat down thankfully as Barbara leant over to them, 'Good old Porter,' she whispered, 'Golly I wouldn't like to be in Miss Winter's shoes.' The first form mistress shot the girl a stern look, but there was a twinkle in her eye. Nan smiled hopefully; perhaps drama lessons would be more endurable from now on.

Porcine Pranks at St. Anne's

Miss Porter did indeed speak to the mistress, and she also let Miss Montagu know of the affair.

The Headmistress was sitting at her desk looking at the sixth form's applications for colleges when Miss Porter knocked.

She looked up, 'Come in!'

The first form mistress entered, shutting the door behind her before advancing into the room.

'Oh, it's you Eileen.'

'I'm not interrupting anything, am I?'

'No, not at all, what's wrong?'

'It's Miss Winter,' said Miss Porter heavily, sitting down in the chair opposite.

'Ah,' sighed Miss Montagu, 'yes, I must say I am not overly impressed by her, but she was all I could find at such short notice,' she spoke as one who had bought something disappointing from a store, 'What's she been doing?'

'From what I can gather she has been using her position of power to dominate Nan Miller, among others,' said Miss Porter damningly, 'getting her to waste time doing her hair for no reason at all that I can see and I'm sure there's more. When I spoke to her about it -and I was very polite- she was exceedingly sullen and the way she talked of Nan you would have supposed her to be doing nothing else but cause trouble which, of course is nonsense; Nan is one of the most hard-working members of her form. Not one of the other mistresses can stand her,' she added, concerned, 'there's something sly and spiteful about her somehow.'

'Um,' mused Miss Montagu, 'well, this is most unfortunate. I have a candidate for next term, but she can't possibly leave her current post until then. If we could just hang onto Miss Winter, her contract runs out at the end of this term, when we can be rid of her. Keep an eye on her, won't you, and make sure she doesn't cause any more trouble for Nan Miller?'

Miss Porter nodded, 'I'll certainly try.'

'If she does anything concrete, we shall just have to manage without her somehow, but hopefully this will blow over.' The Headmistress of St. Anne's was notoriously optimistic.

Miss Porter looked a good deal more doubtful but said nothing more.

Nan and Poppy turned up as bidden at break, but the first form mistress seemed surprised to see them.

'Oh, that,' she smiled when they explained, 'I'll go over the lesson tomorrow in prep.. I'm not sure the others understood much of it. I don't want to cut into your break. Nan!' she added suddenly as the two friends made gratefully for the door, 'I have spoken with your drama mistress about treating all members of the form equally; if she gives you any more trouble you will tell me won't you?'

Nan nodded fervently although secretly she couldn't help feeling a little doubtful. Some things could seem so small as to feel hardly worth reporting. Sometimes one began to doubt oneself, to think perhaps one was imagining things. But small things build up into big worries. And there was always the worry that reporting anything would only make the drama mistress vengeful. Oh, dear, it was difficult!

'Come on,' said Poppy's voice in her ear, 'Let's go and practice some Lacrosse shots.'

∽ 10 ∾

Discovery!

After break was sewing with Miss Whyte. The first formers had their sewing lessons around a large polished wooden table, windows either side letting in as much natural light as possible for the intricate work. The girls were each working on embroidering a set of plain white handkerchiefs. Several of them were struggling including Poppy who was very heavy handed with her needle. She would tug and tug at it and then suddenly it would fly through almost stabbing Beryl, who sat next to her, in the eye.

'Sorry,' said Poppy sheepishly the third time this happened.

'Gracious!' exclaimed Miss Whyte, alarmed, 'I think perhaps we ought to leave the chair to Pamela's right empty. We don't want any accidents.' Beryl got to her feet with alacrity.

Barbara and Daisy-May sewed well but rather slowly and Elaine was almost as bad as Poppy. Nan and Sarah were by far the best in the class.

'I don't know how you do it,' grumbled Poppy, peering over at her friend's beautifully neat pattern of all different flowers dancing around the length of the border.

'Well, I suppose it's in my blood,' said Nan modestly, her needle moving in and out of the cotton fabric with effortless grace, leaving behind a trail of fine coloured silk. 'My father is a tailor and my mother a seamstress. That's how they met when they lived in London. Then they fell in love and started their own dressmaker's business.'

'Really?' gaped Poppy, 'Well no wonder you're so good. Golly, so they must make all your clothes then?'

'Yes,' said Nan enthusiastically, 'I get to choose the pattern and the material, it's grand fun. I have made a few of my own things as well, but they're not nearly so good.'

Just then Wang Li let out a shout of pain and stood up abruptly. Leonora, who sat next to her, stood up as well.

'You stabbed me in the leg, you clumsy idiot!' cried Wang Li, 'And look! What's this?'

'Winifred, Leonie,' fluttered Miss Whyte, 'Whatever's happened here?'

Looking down at her skirt, the Chinese girl saw that Leonora had conscientiously sewn her handkerchief onto it. And that was not all; Leonora herself was also sporting part of the handkerchief, the result being that the two were joined at the hip like Siamese twins.

Wang Li stared in horror, her eyes widening as she took in the full extent of Leonora's handiwork.

'Terribly sorry old thing,' mumbled Leonora apologetically, 'I never have been any good at needlework.'

'Remind me not to sit next to you in future,' said Wang Li tartly, folding her arms.

'Winifred, Leonie,' fluttered Miss Whyte, 'Whatever's happened here?'

'Leonora's sewn her and Wang Li together,' summarised Barbara in her forthright way.

'Good Lord! What a thing to do!' cried the sewing mistress. Leaping up with surprising energy, she came towards the unhappy pair, a pair of large, sharp, sewing scissors in her hand, her eyes curiously unfocused. 'I'll soon get you apart, now don't worry.'

'Um…Actually, Miss Whyte, I think we'll just go and get Matron,' murmured Leonora faintly, before making for the door, dragging Wang Li with her.

It was a wonder the two girls didn't fall over as they hurried along the corridor in search of the matron of School House, trying to synchronise their steps.

Discovery!

Before they could reach Matron Minton's domain, however, a study door opened and Mamzelle Meuhourat came out, followed by Miss Porter. Mamzelle's eyes almost fell out of her head as she saw the predicament the two girls had managed to get themselves into. Miss Porter recovered quicker, steering the pair inside the study and setting about them with the scissors.

'Well, and whose work is this?' she inquired sarcastically.

'It was Leonora,' replied Wang Li curtly, flashing the girl a reproachful look.

'Indeed?' The thought flashed through the first form mistress' mind that she wouldn't put it past the girl to make such a mess on purpose as a trick. Then again she did hate sewing and she looked contrite enough, although looks, as Miss Porter knew well, could be deceiving. 'Well, I'm sorry Leonora, but it seems you've a lot of work to redo. There,' she added as she cut through the final thread, freeing the two first formers.

Leonora accepted the sorry remains of her late handkerchief from her form mistress, and, with mumbled thanks, departed with Wang Li.

Mamzelle Meuhourat was wiping tears of silent laughter from her cheeks, 'Oh,' she gasped, 'This Leonora, assuredly she will be the death of me as you say in this country! First, she gives to me the halloocinasions, then she sews herself up like a parcel!'

Porcine Pranks at St. Anne's

'What hallucinations?' asked Miss Porter sharply, pricking up her ears at the word.

'Oh, she makes me to believe she is a pig, the wicked girl!' revealed Mamzelle, temporarily off her guard.

'A pig?' echoed the first form mistress, thinking that she must have misheard, 'Why on Earth would you think Leonora were a pig, Delphine?'

'Because there was a pig,' asserted Mamzelle indignantly, 'It was sitting at her desk, I assure you. It spoke with her voice- but, oh, it was such a trick!'

Miss Porter looked astonished, 'But, Delphine, where is this pig now?' she asked with a curious feeling that she were in some strange dream.

'Now?' said Mamzelle, her mouth falling open. She looked about her as if expecting to see the piglet hiding somewhere in the study. 'Alas, I do not know.'

'You don't know?' Miss Porter clutched at her head, 'Well, whyever not? A pig can't just disappear into thin air!'

Mamzelle shuffled her big feet awkwardly.

'You don't mean to say you let them off scott free? And that there's a pig roaming the school grounds unchecked?'

Mamzelle looked stung, 'Who is this Scott? Scott is a boys' name,' she objected sullenly.

'Sometimes, Delphine, I really do despair!' said Miss Porter only half jokingly.

Discovery!

'But the good Engleesh girls they work si dur. It is only natural that they have a bit of fun now and again. Besides, I do not let them off. Leonora, I give her such a scolding that the poor child is in tears!' lied Mamzelle unashamedly.

Miss Porter raised a sceptical eyebrow at this, then sighed and said, 'Very well, I see that I shall just have to do a little detective work of my own.'

Miss Porter's idea of detective work was to tackle the first formers after prep. that night. By the time she reached the first form classroom, however, Miss Knight, who was taking prep. that day had already dismissed them. Deciding to tackle Leonora about the elusive pig, feeling sure that she would know everything that there was to know, Miss Porter made her way to Miss Sparks' House.

The first formers were very surprised to see their form mistress entering their common room and the mistress was very surprised to note that Leonora Jameson was not among those present.

'Where is Leonora, Flora?' she asked of a tall, blond-haired girl. Flora, who could guess very well where her friend was, did not reply.

'She went for a walk in the grounds,' piped up Agnes at the same moment as Millicent said, 'She told me she was going to the lavatory.'

'Thank you, girls, you have been most helpful,' said Miss Porter, her voice dripping with sarcasm, before heading off briskly to her own house, for she had just remembered how close Leonora and Barbara were.

The mistress reached the common room just in time to see Leonora with one leg over the sill preparing to depart. The first formers of Miss Sparks' having a window opposite, they had signalled the danger.

'Leonora, don't leave us,' implored Miss Porter reproachfully, then, getting straight to the point, 'I would like a word. Mamzelle Meuhourat has been telling me the most fantastic story involving a pig. Where is it?'

The first formers exchanged horrified glances.

'She's in the box room, Miss Porter,' confessed Poppy in a small voice.

'Show me.'

Poppy disappeared with the mistress and the others waited in melancholy silence until they returned.

Presently, the door opened, and the mistress reappeared, a depressed Poppy behind her, clasping tightly to Bobby.

'You will all see Miss Montagu first thing tomorrow morning,' said the first form mistress crisply, 'Leonora you know very well the penalty for breaking the school rules; you are confined to the school grounds until I say otherwise, and, from now on, I think it might be a good thing for you to sit on the front row in lessons, don't you?'

Discovery!

'Yes, Miss Porter,' moaned Leonora miserably.

'Poppy, give Bobby to me.'

Miss Porter attempted to prise Bobby from Poppy's grasp, but the girl hung on desperately. 'I'll make sure that she is taken good care of,' the mistress assured her in a kinder tone, 'I'll visit the kitchens and make sure they know we've got an extra mouth to feed. Trust me, Poppy, Bobby will be much better off now.'

The girl let go, tears running down her cheeks. Nan, seeing her friend's distress put a comforting arm around her and led her to a chair.

'I suppose you were all in on the secret of Bobby's presence here?' asked Miss Porter, turning to Daisy-May.

The head girl studied her shoes intently, 'Yes, Miss Porter. At least, well, no, actually, Elaine Wilson didn't know,' she corrected herself.

The first form mistress raised an eyebrow at this but no one felt like enlightening her on why this was, so she sighed and addressed Daisy-May chidingly, 'As head girl, I would have expected you to advise Poppy to come to me. You know very well that all pets must have written permission and a certificate from the vet what if Bobby had fallen ill? What would you have done then?'

Daisy-May hung her head and Nan felt guiltily that she ought to have done something too and she couldn't help feeling relieved that Bobby was going to be looked after properly from now on.

Porcine Pranks at St. Anne's

It was a dispirited band of first formers who went to bed that night.

In the morning, they all trooped along to Miss Montagu's study where the Headmistress lectured them in her low penetrating voice. They were all to go to bed one hour earlier every night for the rest of the half term and they were forbidden from leaving the school grounds this coming weekend- the last one before half term. Normally the Lower School was allowed to venture out at the weekend to the village teashop or to buy any odds and ends they needed. Those in the Upper School were even allowed to ride into town to visit the 'flicks'. Nan, what with looking after Bobby and her Lacrosse practice, had not actually taken advantage of this opportunity yet. Wang Li also had appeared unwilling to leave the school grounds and had generally got Barbara to buy any little thing she needed.

Miss Montagu fixed Poppy with her dark stare as the girl spoke in a rush, 'Miss Montagu, oh please, may I keep Bobby here? Don't send her away! I couldn't bear it if you did, why, I should have to leave too, and-!'

The headmistress put up a hand to stem the flow, giving the girl a reassuring smile, 'Of course, I shall have to obtain your parents' written consent and a certificate of health from the vet, but, if I manage to obtain these two things, I see no reason why Bobby should not stay on at the school. She may have her own little room off the stables; perhaps, if you had warned us of her coming, she could have had her own sty.'

Poppy brightened up considerably once she knew that Bobby would be staying on at St. Anne's.

Meanwhile Miss Porter was as good as her word. Having installed Bobby in the stables in the care of the stable lad and groom, she went straight to the kitchens where she found Cook in the midst of weighing out quantities of flour and sugar in large brass scales.

'Ah, I see you're busy, so I won't keep you. I just wanted to inform you that we have a new arrival in the stables- a piglet. If you could keep back any potato peelings and other vegetable waste for the compost for it.

Understanding dawned on Cook's large rosy face, 'Ah, so that's what it was for...'

She stopped abruptly on seeing the quizzical look on the mistress' face.

'What what was for?'

'Nuffin',' said Cook quickly, 'I didn't say nuffin'. Did I say nuffin', Annie?' she demanded of a harassed looking kitchenmaid who had entered stage left from the pantry.

'No ma'am. Yes, ma'am,' flailed the girl helplessly, shooting intense glances between the two before fleeing like a frightened rabbit.

'Well,' Miss Porter laid a hand on the door handle, 'It's nice to know that it's diet didn't suffer at any rate. I'll leave you to it.'

So saying, the mistress vanished, a smile twitching the corners of her lips, quite unaware of the damage her words had caused to a perfectly good late egg which was now lying in a sorry mess on the kitchen floor.

'That Miss Porter,' grumbled Cook disconsolately, 'Always costs me an egg, she does with her sharp tongue. I ought to start charging her, so I ought.' Then, 'Annie! Get yourself in here and clean up this mess!'

11

The Telegram

The next day, Elaine Wilson came out of the San.. By now the story of the first formers' trick on Mamzelle Meuhourat was all over the school and it wasn't long before it came to Elaine's ears. The girl was furious. So, they had been having fun whilst she was in the San. and not one of them had come to visit her. Elaine did not stop to think why that might be, that she herself could be responsible, or, even, that she had been infectious and so naturally had not been permitted visitors anyhow. All that she could see was that they were going to pay for their meanness in excluding her.

Over the next few days items started to disappear. First Poppy's wristwatch went. The girl hunted for it everywhere but couldn't find it since it was at the back of Elaine Wilson's bedside cabinet. Next to be mislaid was a tin of shortbread that Beryl had been sent by an uncle.

'Blow!' she exclaimed, 'it's my only tuck. I was going to get some more this weekend but as we're not allowed out, I shan't be able to!'

This was the first Elaine had heard of the first formers' punishment as they had, understandably, not seen fit to tell her. This news made the girl very smug indeed.

'You could always ask one of the second formers to get something for you,' suggested Daisy-May reasonably.

'What! Those stuck-up little blighters!' exclaimed Beryl explosively, then lowered her voice as Matron's head hovered in the doorway. 'Not likely. I'll just have to plead with Cook to give me some of her jam tarts.'

'You're so lucky, Beryl,' observed Wang Li enviously, 'I do believe Cook would do anything for you.'

'I can't believe how hungry you get,' stated Barbara, 'You eat twice as much as me at dinner and yet you're still hungry and thin as a rake as well.'

Elaine listened distractedly to this banter, her mind still on Beryl's problem. Why, she could easily ask Elaine herself if she would get her things from the village but no, she'd never ask her, Elaine, a thing like that, thought the girl sullenly. It never occurred to her that perhaps stealing was not the best way to go about making friends.

Porcine Pranks at St. Anne's

Not being allowed out that weekend, the first formers were at a loose end as to what to do. Nan had been roped into a Lacrosse practice with other hopefuls for the Lower School team, but the others were all sat about in the common room.

Closing her books with a snap, Poppy sprang to her feet and hurried into her coat, 'I'm off to pay Bobby a visit. Anyone else coming?'

'I'll come,' said Barbara at once and Wang Li, Beryl and Daisy-May stood up too.

Elaine found herself left alone in the Common Room with the dying embers of the wood fire. Determined not to be left behind, she got to her feet abruptly and followed her classmates outside.

The stables were located through a gate off the gravel path that led down to the three houses -two of which were Miss Porter's and Miss Sparks', the other smaller one being shared by several members of the domestic staff.

The first formers found Bobby deep inside a trough of vegetable peelings mixed with bran mash. Pleasurable grunts and snorts emanated from her, and she gave her mistress' hand only the briefest of licks before returning to the business in hand – or rather in trotter.

In between petting Bobby, the first formers

discussed the coming half term holiday weekend when parents would arrive to take the girls out.

'Are your parents coming Poppy?' asked Barbara, stroking Bobby's soft, delicately haired back affectionately.

'No, they can't very well leave the farm,' replied Poppy, a tad dolefully, 'But my aunt's coming though. What about you?'

'Well, it's just me and Father and he already works next door so we'll probably go out somewhere Saturday and I might join Leonora on the Sunday,' said Barbara happily, 'Are your parents coming Wang Li?'

'Yes, they are coming this time because it is the first half term. They probably won't come every time though since it's so far to go.'

'My parents are coming,' piped up Beryl, holding out an appetising carrot to Bobby, 'We're going into town to see a show at the theatre.'

'We're going for a picnic,' volunteered Daisy- May.

Barbara was looking past them at Elaine Wilson, who she had spotted skulking some little distance away. Elaine's parents won't be coming, thought the girl to herself. If only she were a bit nicer, she could go out with a friend but really, she doesn't do herself any favours.

The week before half term seemed to drag on and on to the excited first formers. All the mistresses were busy picking out work to go on display in the various form rooms. Miss Whyte wanted to display Nan's embroidered handkerchiefs. Nan was very proud of her work and agreed readily on the condition that she could have them back in time to give to her parents.

Nan was also to be part of the Lower School Lacrosse display and would play in an exhibition match on the Saturday. Wang Li's French work in her beautifully neat handwriting was given pride of place by Mamzelle in the first form classroom. Poppy's latest history essay in her large rounded childlike hand was also chosen for praise as was a charming watercolour painting of Beryl's.

Two girls from the Lower School were also to play a piano duet during the welcome assembly for the parents. Beryl and Wang Li were both in the running, of course, being two of the eight Lower School girls to take piano lessons.

One evening they returned from a joint lesson, entering the Common Room in a sort of daze.

'Beryl! Wang Li!' cried Barbara pouncing on them, 'Whatever's up? You look like you've seen a ghost?'

Wang Li sank down into a chair and buried her face in her hands. Beryl sat on the edge of a chair tentatively, her eyes wide and staring.

'Well?' demanded Barbara, 'Spit it out? What in the World's the matter?'

The Telegram

'I do believe she's going to choose me,' whispered Beryl in a sort of awed horror.

'Good luck,' said Wang Li, peeping out briefly from behind her hands.

Beryl groaned, 'but oh, I don't want to play in front of all the parents. Why, I'd go to pieces. And, besides, you're better than I am, Wang Li.'

'Let me get this straight,' said Barbara in business-like tones, 'Miss Winter is going to pick Beryl to play the duet when Wang Li is a better player and Beryl doesn't want to do it, is that right?'

'In a nutshell,' gulped Beryl, 'Oh, what are we to do? I feel terrible for you, Wang Li. The way she kept praising me and finding fault with you! I could have sunk through the floor! And I know you wanted so much to play in front of your parents.'

Wang Li made a face, 'You'll be fine, Beryl, you do it.'

But Beryl shook her head desperately.

Barbara looked from one to the other of them in consternation. What on Earth was to be done?

It was Leonora who provided the answer. Barbara was strolling across the lawn with her at morning break, her mind still on the piano duet puzzle.

'What's wrong with you?' asked Leonora sharply, 'You obviously haven't been paying attention to a word I've been saying. Why, I just said that Mamzelle Mole Rat has moved on from hallucinations and fancies herself a canary, and you didn't even laugh.'

'Sorry,' said Barbara contritely and told her friend of what was on her mind.

'Hmmm,' said Leonora, rubbing a chin between finger and thumb as she always did when putting in a spell of hard thinking, 'Do you know, I've got the glimmer of an idea. You say the lucky pair will be picked at dinner break on Thursday?'

Barbara nodded.

'What we need is to get Miss Winter away from the school for then so that the pianists can be judged fairly. It just so happens that I was outside the school office the other day-'

Barbara raised quizzical eyebrows.

'Just minding my own business, my dear girl,' retorted Leonora smoothly, her mouth twitching suspiciously, 'Anyway, I overheard Miss Winter talking to the secretary. She'd just had a letter from her sister who lives in Northheath. Well, the sister appeared to be quite well, but Miss Winter was worried about her for this was not often the case. She said that she is often taken very badly, and bed ridden for several weeks.'

Barbara was looking thoughtful, 'So, if we were to ring up pretending to be Miss Winter's sister-?'

'Possibly,' allowed Leonora graciously, 'But who's to say Miss Winter wouldn't be called to the 'phone herself.

The Telegram

No, I've got a better idea. We hand in a telegram in the village purporting to come from Miss Winter's sister calling Miss Winter away to Northheath.'

'But do you know her sister's name?' pointed out Barbara shrewdly.

'Mrs Alice Thomas,' grinned Leonora, 'I'm not to be caught out that way; I'm very thorough.'

'So I see,' remarked Barbara drily, 'Go on.'

'Well, it will mean sneaking into the village,' admitted Leonora, 'I shall have to be in mufti, or someone may mention seeing me and report me to Miss Porter and only the two top forms are allowed out during dinner break.'

'Miss Porter will be wild if she finds out,' objected Barbara fretfully.

'She isn't going to find out,' countered Leonora confidently, clapping her friend reassuringly on the shoulder.

The lesson before dinner break on a Thursday was singing with Miss Layton. This was held in the school hall with the second and third forms with the mistress accompanying the children on the piano, so it was an easy matter to slip out quarter of an hour early.

First Leonora went to Miss Sparks' House and, taking off her eye-catching green blazer, put on a long coat and scarf which hid her grey gymslip and gingham dress underneath. Cramming a felt hat on her head in an effort to disguise her short flaming red hair, the girl crept out of the house, through the wooded grounds and out into the lane by way of a handy hole in the hedge.

A short walk took the brazen first former to the village of Hillesley where she approached the general store and post office cautiously. She did not want to run into the post mistress- or any of the St. Anne's mistresses come to that. It was her intention to get the post mistress' son, Fred, alone.

Risking a peep in at the window, Leonora saw to her relief that her luck was in, and Fred had the shop to himself. She entered confidently, the little bell on the door jingling merrily as she did so.

Fred looked up. He was a runner bean of a boy, not very much older than Leonora herself. He appeared to have grown a good deal taller than wider, giving the impression of a head perched on top of a suit of clothes animated to life.

He grinned when he saw Leonora, 'Hullo, what can I do for you? Want another half-pound of toffees? I say, how come you're in mufti, and hang on a minute, it's not the weekend! You're not supposed to be here!'

'Shhh!' hissed Leonora, 'I know, I haven't much time. I need you to take down a telegram quickly and paste it on a form. Now type this out.'

The Telegram

Fred did as he was told though his expression showed clearly his mystification. 'I could get into serious trouble for this you know. Forging telegrams, I don't know. Whatever next,' he complained as he handed Leonora the finished article.

'It was handed in at Northheath Post Office,' stipulated the girl dictatorially.

'Northheath? But I-'

'Write it down.'

Fred did so reluctantly, muttering darkly to himself.

'Thank you,' Leonora smiled sweetly at him, scrawled something in an illegible hand where the signature ought to go and handed it back to Fred. 'There, now mind you give that to the telegraph boy to hand in at the school office at twelve sharp- no later.'

'Yes Miss,' groaned Fred as Leonora turned on her heel and disappeared.

Miraculously Leonora's daredevil plan succeeded. Miss Winter was called away just before dinner break and got the next bus out of the village on the carefully planned wild goose chase. Miss Layton was left to step in and judge the pianists. It was a near thing, five of the eight being deservedly good players, but in the end, the singing mistress picked out Betty Hall from the third form and Zhang Wang Li from the first.

The first formers were triumphant and Miss

'Yes, miss,' groaned Fred as Leonora turned on her heel and disappeared.

The Telegram

Winter, when she had returned from her pointless trip to Northheath as far from gruntled as can readily be imagined.

There remained one thing to be done and that was to destroy the evidence. Leonora had no intention of Fred suffering for her trick. With characteristic audacity, therefore, she entered the school office when the school day was over, and the secretary had gone home. A quick search of the neatly stacked shelves and well-ordered files retrieved the incriminating telegram.

Later, in the Common Room, she thrust it into the brightly roaring log fire and watched as its edges caught alight and crumpled in on themselves until it was gone, reduced to ashes.

12

Elaine's Second Chance

The episode of the peculiar telegram caused for its fair share of mystification and speculation among the students and staff. However, without any evidence and with the excitement of half term looming, it was, for the most part, quickly forgotten about. Wang Li put the incident down to providence and Miss Winter regretfully relinquished any hope of catching the culprit. Barbara, of course, knew who was responsible, but if Leonora wanted it to remain a secret, she was not going to betray her friend's trust.

Half term came at last, and the first formers all sat on the front lawn watching for their parents to arrive. Barbara stood with her father, Professor Wofflespoon, who was tall and thin like her, impeccably dressed in waistcoat and tie and possessed of a peculiarly endearing expression of permanent worry.

Poppy's aunt turned up first, walking briskly from the direction of the village. She wore a neat suit and skirt and carried a large practical handbag. She greeted her niece formally and the two of them went off together, Poppy casting a longing look back at Nan.

Beryl's parents arrived in a glossy sports car which must have been unimaginably draughty, although, Nan noticed, they were well tucked around with blankets. Daisy-May's parents also came by motor car, but they were in a sensibly enclosed Morris Cowley.

Nan's parents walked up deep in conversation with a short, smiling, dark haired couple whom Nan had little difficulty in recognising as the parents of Wang Li. Her own parents were sensibly but fashionably dressed and, looking at their happy, interested faces, Nan felt a thrill of pride for them.

Skipping off to join them Nan was far too absorbed to think about Elaine Wilson still sitting forlornly on the damp grass. Barbara saw her, however, and frowned. Thinking back to their dormitory and all the family photographs displayed on the girls' bedside cabinets, she could not remember having seen one of Elaine's parents.

Taking pity on the girl, Barbara tugged at her father's sleeve at exactly the same moment that he remarked in his deep ponderous tones, 'Who's that over there? They don't look very happy, Barbara?'

'That's Elaine, Father. I don't think her parents are coming.'

'What a shame,' remarked the kind-hearted Professor Wofflespoon, 'Would you mind if she tagged along with us?'

'Not at all; I was about to suggest it,' said Barbara and there was a note of determination in her voice. She may be sharp-tongued, but Barbara had inherited her father's kindness. Elaine may ruin her half-term, but Barbara was fed up of seeing her sulking about all over the place. If she had anything to do with it, Elaine would jolly well buck up a bit!

The girl looked up dolefully when Professor Wofflespoon made his offer and Barbara thought for a minute she was about to refuse.

The St. Becket's master, however, heard the doubt in her voice and pressed on, 'We would be delighted to have your company, Elaine, if you have no prior engagements?'

'No,' stuttered Elaine and smiled. Barbara gave a gasp. It was quite amazing what a difference that smile made to the girl's face. Her eyes smiled too, looking sparkly and warm where before they had seemed dull and lifeless.

Elaine was quite overjoyed to be asked out, having quite given up hope of ever going out at half term.

There was no doubt about it; Professor Wofflespoon was a hit with Elaine. Barbara would have felt quite left out if she hadn't been busy marvelling at the change in her classmate.

Parents and students made a tour of school and grounds, visiting everywhere from the kitchen garden to the laboratory to the coal cellar. It took a while for Elaine to find her tongue. At first, she merely listened to Barbara's father with rapt attention as he related hilarious tales from his time teaching at St. Becket's. Later, however, she chattered on animatedly about incidents which had taken place in one of the half a dozen or so scholastic establishments she appeared to have attended before her current spell at St. Anne's.

Nan enjoyed the Saturday immensely. The only damper on things was that her carefully embroidered handkerchiefs, that she had been so looking forward to showing her parents, had disappeared and were nowhere to be found.

'Never mind, dear,' said Mrs Miller, seeing the downcast expression on her daughter's face. 'I'm sure they'll turn up sooner or later and we can see them when you bring them home at the end of term.'

Nan tried to look happier and had soon forgotten all about this disappointment when she managed to set up a goal for a second former in the Lower School

Porcine Pranks at St. Anne's

Lacrosse Display. Nan intercepted a clumsy pass by a third former, catching the ball neatly in her net, before running the length of the pitch and lobbing it to a well-placed teammate who sent it spinning into the opponents' goal.

The first formers joined in a raucous cheering for their classmate and Nan was giddy with happiness for the rest of the day.

After her bracing bout of fresh air, Nan was ravenous and acquiesced eagerly when her father suggested that they pay a visit to the village teashop. Mr Miller was a tall well-build man with an easy grace, which combined with his impeccable taste in clothing gave him a debonair air that made Nan very proud to be seen alongside him. He also had a sweet tooth. His wife disapproved of this quality and steadfastly refused to bake for him at home, so he always filled himself up on sweet treats when out and about.

'I'll have a chocolate éclair, please,' he said now, eyes twinkling mischievously as Beatrice, the languid waitress of the China Pot Tea Shop took laborious notes. Nan's mother pursed her lips.

'Just sandwiches and tea for me, please,' she said.

'Could I have a scone, please?' asked Nan, swinging her legs under the table and smiling at her parents.

'With jam, Miss?' inquired Beatrice in bored tones.

'And cream. Don't forget the cream,' stipulated Mr

Miller and earned himself a reproachful look from his wife.

Looking contentedly around the cosy little teashop with its dimmed orange lights and squashy cushions, Nan noticed Poppy and her aunt at a small table by the window. Poppy was staring enviously over at Nan's family and could only manage a strained smile when Nan gave her a bright grin.

By the time the two first formers and their people had finished their tea the sky outside had darkened to a dolphin grey hue and an impish wind was picking up handfuls of fallen leaves to hurl across the ground. A persistent rain beat a steady pattern on the windowpanes.

'Lucky I brought an umbrella,' remarked Nan's mother, ever resourceful. Poppy's aunt, too, drew out a large black umbrella from the recesses of her handbag, like a magician producing a rabbit from a hat.

The two families hurried back up the lane that led to the school gates together, their feet plashing through the shallow puddles. They made it, flushed and damp, just in time to take their places in the assembly hall with the other students and parents.

Miss Montagu stood at the lectern and addressed those assembled in her clear, mellifluous voice, welcoming parents and girls and commenting on the start of the academic year. Isobel Harding said a word or two and then a handful of Upper School girls came up one by one to give a short recital, sing or play a piece on the piano. Finally, it was the turn of the Lower School girls and Nan saw Wang Li edge onto the stage alongside Betty Hall. They sat down at the piano and proceeded to play The Celebrated Chop Waltz written in 1877. It was a lively piece, filling the packed hall with rich sonorous notes that followed each other at an impressive pace.

As the last note faded away everyone clapped heartily and the two girls retook their seats, blushing.

Refreshments followed before it was time to say goodbye until the morning.

Nan and Poppy awoke early, dressed in printed cotton frocks and sat helping each other do their hair.

'Nan,' began Poppy after a while, 'My Aunt can't come today. Do you think I could tag along with you?'

'Of course,' said Nan at once, thankful that Poppy would not be stuck with her prim aunt for the whole of the half-term holiday.

'I say,' continued Poppy doubtfully, 'do you think your parents would mind awfully if I brought Bobby along?'

'No, not at all,' smiled Nan, overjoyed at the prospect of having the piglet for company, 'They love animals.'

And so Poppy and her unusual pet accompanied the Miller family on their picnic. The two girls ran on ahead with Bobby, the adults following with the wicker hamper.

After a couple of miles across country the little group came upon a small mound of a hill which, on being climbed, presented the most marvellous views on all sides. In the distance the quirky ruins of Hillesley Castle were clearly visible along with the imposing landmarks of the two schools.

It was a good day for a picnic. Although there was a slight nip in the air, there was very little breeze and the sun's rays beat down with a gentle warmth.

Everyone flopped down on the picnic rug that Mrs Miller had thoughtfully brought along, tired out from their walk. Poppy's eyes gleamed as Nan's father opened the hamper to reveal cucumber and jam sandwiches, apples, salad, hard-boiled eggs, sausage rolls, big slabs of seedy bread and butter and crumbling slices of fruitcake. They all tucked in hungrily as Bobby frisked about from one to the other demanding any scraps.

'Sausage roll, Nan?' asked her father, holding out the plateful.

Nan looked up at him and Bobby behind him, nosing an apple and felt suddenly quite nauseous. She realised that she had been subconsciously avoiding the sausage rolls and now she saw plainly why.

'Sausage roll, Nan?' asked her father, holding out the plateful.

'No, thank you,' she managed to get out and took a cucumber sandwich instead.

Nan watched Poppy furtively as she attacked a sausage roll seemingly unaware of anything wrong. Having grown up on a farm, Nan supposed Poppy was used to it.

Meanwhile Wang Li and her parents were spending their morning exploring the castle ruins, as were the Wofflespoons and Elaine. Leonora and her parents had rushed off into town to see a play and have dinner at a hotel, but now that she had Elaine for company Barbara didn't mind.

'These ruins date to the time of the English civil war when the castle as a stronghold of the Royalists was besieged and eventually destroyed by Cromwell's Roundheads,' Professor Wofflespoon was saying whilst Elaine drunk in every word, enthralled.

'Here you can see what would have been one of the fireplaces,' pointed out the St. Becket's master, directing Elaine's gaze to an archway at head height framing a hollow in the stonework. 'And up there one can see the same thing recreated in the upper stories,' he added. Everyone craned their necks to see the architectural feature surviving the ruins.

It was very hard, however, to imagine the castle as it had once been. The wooden floors had burnt away,

Porcine Pranks at St. Anne's

leaving only ridges to determine the height of the ceiling and the green grass that carpeted the ground was very different from the floorboards and woven rugs there had once been.

As St. Becket's half-term coincided with St Anne's and most of the boys were out with their parents for the day, Professor Wofflespoon was able to take the two first formers back to his house to eat. It was over dinner that Elaine broke down. She sobbed for all she was worth. Barbara smiled at her reassuringly and Professor Wofflespoon patted her hand, not sure what else to do.

Eventually Elaine subsided enough to be able to talk. 'I'm sorry,' she gulped, 'you've just been so kind to me. I've been so lonely always you don't know what it means. After Mother and Father moved back to Hong Kong, I've just been passed from one school to another. They wrote occasionally but they've only come to visit once. At first, I tried to make friends, but I was so jealous of everyone else. And I can't bear to think of how mean I've been to you all.'

'Oh Elaine!' said Barbara, putting an arm around the girl's shoulders, 'it's silly to be jealous. It doesn't hurt anyone but yourself.'

'Yes, I know that now,' admitted Elaine looking very ashamed, 'Oh, Barbara, how awful I've been! How I hated you all!'

'It was you who let Bobby out, wasn't it?' asked Barbara accusingly.

Elaine nodded, 'Yes, and I stole those things of yours. I didn't do anything with them though. They're still in my bedside cabinet.'

'You stole from the first form last term as well, didn't you?' pressed Barbara, as her father looked on, mildly inquisitive.

Elaine bit her lip, 'Yes.'

'And you were almost expelled but were given a second chance. And now you've gone and blown that, Oh Elaine!'

The first former looked horrified. 'Oh, no, but I won't be expelled, will I?'

Barbara looked at her steadily. She felt sorry for the girl. She may have been silly and spiteful, but she had never had the steadying influence of supportive parents. Barbara blamed them entirely for the pickle Elaine had got herself in. 'That's for the rest of the form to decide,' she said grimly.

Elaine said nothing. She did not hold out much hope that the other first formers would want anything more to do with her, but she knew that she had brought everything on herself and must have the courage to face the consequences, however unpleasant.

'I'm sure everything will turn out all right,' put in Professor Wofflespoon optimistically.

13

A Trial and a Tea

The rest of the first formers were surprised to be called to a meeting in the Common Room on returning to St. Anne's. There was still a half-term tea to look forward to after all. However, whilst their parents were busy talking with their various mistresses, the first formers filed curiously into the Common Room.

Elaine was almost in tears, but, with occasional help from Barbara, she managed to tell her story and the stolen things were handed back. Poppy's wristwatch, Beryl's shortbread, Nan's handkerchief and a book of Barbara's that she hadn't even realised was missing.

No one was particularly surprised that Elaine had been the one behind the mysterious disappearances. Although initially there were expressions of disgust

A Trial and a Tea

and exclamations of scorn, the first formers all began to feel uncomfortable as Barbara told Elaine's story. Not one of them had ever really tried to get to the bottom of the girl's gloom or help her in any way. Now they couldn't help feeling sorry for her. After all being abandoned at such a young age to go from one school to another, spending all one's holidays at school must be hateful.

Nan was just overjoyed to have her embroidery work back again- she would be able to give them to her parents after all.

'Hands up who thinks Elaine should be given a fresh start?' said Daisy-May, taking charge.

Barbara, Wang Li, Nan and Beryl put up their hands at once. Poppy, who was still sore about Elaine's letting Bobby loose, wavered, then followed suit. Daisy-May added her vote, meaning that the first formers were in unanimous agreement to give Elaine another chance.

The girl's face flushed with pleasure, 'Oh thank you so much. I've done nothing to deserve it I know, but you won't regret it, I promise.'

'We had better not,' grated Poppy, 'and you had better not try any more tricks on Bobby.'

'Of course not,' cried Elaine, going red with shame, 'Oh Poppy, I'm so sorry. I'll make it up to you. I'll take Bobby her bran mash and vegetable peelings every dinner break, I will.'

Porcine Pranks at St. Anne's

Poppy looked somewhat mollified at this and gave the girl a small smile.

'That's the spirit, Elaine,' enthused Barbara, slapping her on the back, 'that ought to keep you busy; we don't want you doing any more moping around, you know.'

'Yes,' put in Beryl, 'if I catch you dragging your heels, I'll send you off to Nan for Lacrosse practice.'

Elaine shivered slightly at this prospect for what with the nights drawing in and Winter on its way, it was very cold and bleak indeed outside. Lacrosse practice in such conditions might be Nan's cup of tea but it certainly wasn't Elaine's. Yet somehow or other Nan always managed to come back radiating an energy and heat that not even the common room fire could equal.

Suddenly there came a fierce ringing and the first formers leapt to their feet eagerly. 'Teatime! At last!' cried Poppy.

'And not just any teatime,' Barbara reminded her, 'it's still half-term and the kitchen staff always pull their socks up to impress the parents.'

Sure enough the tables were groaning with sumptuous goodies of all kinds. There were sandwiches and huge salads, cold meats, glistening fruit cakes, Victoria sandwiches, oozing jam and cream, dishes of strawberries and raspberries and enormous trifles,

A Trial and a Tea

their layers distinct through the glass bowls. The dining room was twice as busy as usual with the parents as excited by the magnificent spread as the girls.

Nan, slipping into the place between her parents, thought her father to be in a seventh heaven of delight. For once her mother seemed resigned to the fact that he would 'overeat himself' as she called it. Poppy and Beryl, sitting on his other side, tucked in with the same gusto and conversation was limited.

On the other side of the table, Zhang Chen and Tang Zhi Ruo were sampling the food cautiously. They appeared particularly bemused by the trifle and Nan supposed that they must never have seen one before. Nan was quite fascinated by the Zhang family and had to be careful not to appear to be staring. They conversed with their daughter in English for the most part but occasionally they broke into Mandarin Chinese. Her parents seemed to address Wang Li as something that sounded to Nan's untrained ears as Shaw Shong Maw. She supposed it must be a nickname and made a mental note to ask her classmate about it later.

Wang Li was bright-eyed with pleasure for her parents were relating to her their interviews with her various teachers and all the mistresses had been unanimous in their praise for her. The surly Miss Winter had, it transpired, retired to bed with a headache and so had avoided meeting any of the first formers' parents.

Porcine Pranks at St. Anne's

A turn of events which they, had they known her, would have felt extremely grateful for.

Anyway, the other mistresses had only praise for the Chinese girl. Mamzelle Meuhourat had been delighted to meet Wang Li's parents and had spent so long chatting with them in a flamboyant French that Barbara's father had hardly any of his five-minute slot left. Miss Knight had been so enthusiastic about Wang Li's improved Lacrosse technique that her mother had been inspired to have a go herself (they had been on the front lawn at the time) and had very almost taken her husband's eye out.

'No, no, Lao Tang,' insisted Wang Li's father smilingly, 'Your mother is exaggerating Xiao Xiong Mao; the stick was nowhere near me.'

'It was,' contested his wife, hotly, 'it was your father standing too close. But what a peculiar game this Lacrosse is. We were most impressed by the demonstration yesterday. Nan Miller, your friend who I see is sitting opposite us, she performed outstandingly for a first former. And such an exciting game; I wouldn't mind taking it up myself.'

Wang Li's father looked alarmed at this prospect and quickly steered the conversation into more convivial waters, 'Your form mistress, Miss Porter, impressed us very much and she was singing your praises.'

'Yes,' added Mrs Zhang emotionally, 'Porter Laoshi said she was in awe of your language skills, Xiao Xiong Mao.'

A Trial and a Tea

Wang Li blushed with pleasure and embarrassment as she allowed her mother to embrace her.

It was late by the time the first formers dragged tired feet up the stairs to bed. Emotional goodbyes had been said and they had waved their parents off into the cold dark night and watched headlamps beam on before swinging off, away from the school.

Now Matron, who appeared half-asleep herself, was fussing about, hovering impatiently whilst the first formers got ready for bed.

'Oh, Wang Li,' exclaimed Nan, as she rummaged about for her tooth paste tin, 'I was going to ask you, why do your parents call you Shaw Shong Maw? Is it your nickname?'

For a second the Chinese girl looked bewildered, then her face broke into a grin, 'Oh, Xiao Xiong Mao! Yes, it is a name they call me. It means Little Panda.'

'My parents call me Munchkin,' volunteered Beryl, through a mouthful of toothpaste.

This was a new word for Wang Li, 'It means cute?' she asked once it had been explained, 'In Chinese we say ke ài.'

At this point Matron decided to step in and the girls finished brushing their teeth in silence. 'Lights out now,' boomed Matron from the door, and, stifling an enormous yawn, she was gone.

Porcine Pranks at St. Anne's

Elaine snuggled down between the sheets, glad of the extra blankets for it was a chilly night. Lying, staring up at the whitewashed ceiling, Elaine cast her mind back over the last two days. What fun she had had, and how much better she felt now that she was on the same side as her classmates. She was not a naturally malicious girl and now that she had been shown kindness, she could see clearly how silly she had been. She was now determined to be sensible and enjoy herself with the others. Thinking forward to all the fun that lay ahead of her, Elaine hugged herself ecstatically. Soon, though, her eyelids grew heavy, and she fell into a deep contented sleep.

~ 14 ~

A Discussion Over Dinner

The mistresses were very surprised by the sudden change in Elaine Wilson. She seemed to have gone almost overnight from a sulky, disinterested child to a sparkly-eyed child, brimming over with a newfound joy of life.

Miss Porter having already been the girl's form mistress for a term was familiar with the old Elaine and amazed at her transformation. She couldn't explain it; she just hoped that it was permanent.

Now that Elaine had relinquished the past and was living for the present, she threw herself into lessons and even Lacrosse, though nothing would induce her to practice outside of games lessons. Instead, Elaine spent her free time in the common room where she proved herself a talented dancer. The other first formers were quite as taken aback as the mistresses at the change in her and laughed with her about it good-humouredly.

Along with her attitude, Elaine's appetite also seemed to have improved. She fairly shovelled the food down at dinner time, her cheeks a healthy rosy colour.

Nan, however, was aghast to discover that dinner was sausages and mash. At the sight and smell of the sausages, Nan's stomach turned. Glancing surreptitiously at the others, Nan saw that all of them, apart from Barbara, were tucking in, oblivious. Barbara and her father were vegetarians.

Seeing Nan's face and reading her expression, Barbara said gently, 'Don't eat it if you don't want to.'

'Aren't you hungry, Nan?' asked Beryl at once.

'It's just that I don't think I can eat pork any more, not after spending so much time with Bobby,' explained Nan.

The others looked at each other uncomfortably as if she had just voiced an unpalatable truth that they didn't want to contemplate.

'What is pork,' asked Wang Li, breaking the silence.

'What you're eating,' said Beryl, shortly.

'Oh, zhū ròu; pigs' meat,' Wang Li's face cleared, and Nan realised what a difference a name can make to how you see things.

'Growing up on a farm,' remarked Poppy suddenly, embarking on a speech, 'it's our reality. We care for the animals and make sure that they have a good life, but everyone's got to die sometime and at least they are put to good use. Of course, it's soul-wrenching when they're your friends but at least you've known them, and you respect them. Not eating your own animals, well, I mean, you don't know who you're eating do you?'

Beryl wrinkled her nose and Daisy-May put down her fork.

'Oh dear,' flustered Poppy, 'I've said something wrong, haven't I?'

Beryl stabbed a forkful of sausage, 'I'm so hungry, Poppy, I don't care what I eat, but this is so delicious, I don't think I could become a vegetarian even if I wanted to- the temptation is just too great!'

Poppy looked relieved but Barbara was frowning, 'Of course, none of us can think of eating Bobby. But you can't make exceptions like that. It's no different with any other animal.'

Nan knew that Barbara was right. It was Bobby that had made her first question eating meat, but the same rule must be applied to any other sort of meat.

'In China, my grandmother used to cook us pigs' trotters,' piped up Wang Li in a dubious attempt to be helpful.

'Trotters?' echoed Beryl, 'But surely they've hardly any meat on them?'

'Waste not want not,' put in Poppy, 'if you are going to keep animals then you have to make use of all of them...'

Nan tried to block out her friend's words. Her head was spinning, and a nauseating warmth had risen to the back of her throat. She became aware that Barbara was speaking to her, 'Don't eat anything that makes you uncomfortable, Nan, because there's nothing worse than eating something and then wishing that you hadn't. well, I mean, there are heaps of things worse than that, but you know what I mean- figure of speech and all that. Personally, I've never known what it is that people see in meat- the texture and smell and taste just don't attract me. Ultimately, though, I think everyone's different and we've all just got to make our own minds up for ourselves.'

Nan nodded and ate a tentative forkful of mashed potato, carefully skirting the offending sausage, which Poppy promptly removed for her.

Mamzelle Meuhourat, who had listened to this philosophical discussion in a busy silence, her jaws working almost non-stop, now leant over to Nan and patted her on the shoulder, 'Ah, Nan, ma Cherie, you are sensitive like Barbara. Me, I do not have such qualms, I am a meat-eater.'

A Discussion Over Dinner

This was such an unexpected remark that Nan stared. The French mistress flashed her a toothy grin that showed off so many teeth that for a moment Nan had the impression of talking to a great white shark.

'If we were stranded on a desert island,' continued Mamzelle seriously, 'I would eat you all up. Oh, yes, I would commence with Beryl because she is the juiciest, n'est-ce pas? Barbara and Wang Li, they are so thin and bony, I would eat them last.' The first formers roared at this and Mamzelle winked at Nan who joined in the laughter happily.

15

Mamzelle and the Ghost of St Anne's

The first week after half term went by. Pumpkins, looking all plump and orange, were harvested from the vegetable garden and given over to the kitchens, from whence poured a seemingly endless supply of soup.

'I'm sure I can feel it sloshing about inside me,' complained Leonora, 'Any more and I shouldn't be surprised to find that I've turned into a pumpkin!'

'Well, you're halfway there already,' joked Barbara wryly, tugging at her friend's bob of thick red hair.

Leonora gave her a friendly push before changing the subject abruptly, 'it's ages since we played that trick on Mamzelle Mole Rat. I vote we play her another- she needs a good laugh; she hates this cold weather.'

Nan smiled drily at this- she was sure that Mamzelle would be the one being laughed at.

'What'll we do?' asked Barbara.

'Ooh! Leonora,' squealed Elaine, who had just come in. The first formers were in the bathroom off the dormitory, Leonora with them despite her warning from Miss Porter. 'Oh, yes, do play a trick! I missed the last one and I'm simply longing to be part of one! I feel I should burst with laughter.'

'Well, you had better not,' said Leonora sternly, 'Or it would be a very short trick. Mamzelle may be gullible but even she would soon smell a rat if you started with hysterics five minutes in.'

'I'll try not to,' promised Elaine seriously, 'But, oh, I'm so excited!'

'We might get the fake chalk out again,' continued Leonora, ignoring her, 'Miss Winter never reported that, so Mamzelle won't be on her guard. And I think we could definitely use that invisible string again. I need to think it out, but I thought we could do something ghostly.'

The first formers had a French literary lesson every Friday and, having finished a short play, they had now embarked on a ghost story which the girls found hilarious, but which seemed to affect Mamzelle pretty badly.

'That's a wizard idea,' said Nan heartily, her eyes shining in anticipation of the trick.

Porcine Pranks at St. Anne's

Suddenly Barbara gave a little gasp, 'I say, I've just thought,' she explained, 'if we read ahead, we could plan the tricks to mirror the plot of the story!'

'Who can possibly read ahead in all that terribly boggy French?' argued Leonora derisively.

'Wang Li can,' stated Barbara just as Wang Li herself entered and began vigorously applying soap to her face.

'Did I hear my name?' she asked, her face a comical mask of lather. Quickly Leonora put Barbara's idea to her. Wang Li agreed readily, all too keen for some more fun and everything was settled.

Wang Li spent the next evening in the common room curled up in one of the big armchairs, reading through the next chapter and making a note in an old exercise book of the various ghostly occurrences which took place. Nan, leaning over her shoulder, was amazed at the way she switched between languages, at times copying down the French, jotting down the Chinese when a word escaped her and going back and inserting the English when it came to her.

'You're a genius,' breathed Nan, 'I don't know how you do it.'

Wang Li laughed, 'You would be just as good if you were forced to speak French or Chinese to be understood. When you are immersed in a language you pick it up much easier. Anyway, this is pretty unintelligible as it is.

I'll have to put it all into English for Leonora. But Nan, there's so much scope here; I can't wait for Friday!'

Wang Li gave Leonora her notes and she and Barbara disappeared to the dormitory and Leonora's secret stash of tricks that she kept under a loose floorboard near Barbara's bed, where they planned meticulously.

When at last Friday came, the first formers could hardly wait for afternoon lessons and drove Miss Knight and Miss Sparks to distraction, staring glassily out of windows and bursting out with smothered giggles for no apparent reason.

Whilst their classmates spent some of their pent-up energy out on the Lacrosse field at dinner break, Barbara and Leonora made their way to the first form classroom and planted their tricks. These consisted of a length of invisible string tied around the lock of the sash window which ran onto the floor and under the desks to Leonora's chair. Then there was a balloon blown up and stoppered with a cork affixed to another length of string which ran to Leonora chair also. Rolling up a sleeve of her cardigan, Barbara took the balloon and managed to place it a little way up the chimney where there was a handy ledge for just such occasions as these.

Barbara drew her arm out again hastily, grimacing at the fine dusting of soot that now coated it. Luckily there was a lavatory nearby. Leonora checked the coast was clear before urging her friend out. Barbara skipped along and had almost reached the bathroom when Miss Knight came along through the corridor from the back stairs. The first former hurriedly hid her right arm behind her back.

'Hello, Barbara,' said the young mistress merrily, 'I've just marked your history homework, if you want it back?' but Barbara, becoming desperate, suddenly omitted an alarming retching sound and, putting her left hand up to her mouth, dashed into the bathroom, her right arm still hidden from view.

Miss Knight stood for a moment before following the girl, a concerned look on her face. She entered the room just in time to see Barbara drying off her hands at the washbasin.

'Are you all right? Should I fetch Matron?' she asked.

'Perfectly. Never better,' replied the mischievous first former breezily, 'there's really no need, Miss Knight. Did you say something about history homework?'

Miss Knight blinked. Really, these first formers were such queer things.

At long last the bell for afternoon school sounded and the first formers' chatter died as they rose as one at Nan's signal from the door. Mamzelle Meuhourat's high heels click clacked on the wooden floor before she appeared in the doorway.

'Merci bien, Nan, ma chérie,' she said, her voice sounding hoarse. Seating herself at the desk, she seemed to sag into the chair like a sack of potatoes, 'Ah mes enfants!' she wailed, 'this weather, he does not agree with me. Always in Switzerland it was the same, but there at least we had the snow. La neige, c'était tellement belle! But here you have the wet!'

Leonora nodded sagely, amused at Mamzelle's little outburst.

'Ah, but you are children. You have not my bones! You wait till you have my bones!' Nan and Poppy exchanged a bemused glance. They very much hoped they would not inherit Mamzelle Meuhourat's troublesome bones.

'Alors!' cried Mamzelle, suddenly straightening to attention in a manner reminiscent of a marionette when its string is pulled, 'Allons-y! Please to take out your French novels and we will continue with la lecture. Beryl, you may read first.'

Beryl didn't appear at all thrilled at this honour and couldn't resist a worried glance back at Leonora. The girl winked back at her encouragingly- the trick was on.

Stumbling over the unfamiliar French, the ghost story didn't sound terribly frightening coming piecemeal out of Beryl's tentative mouth. Leonora hoped very much that Mamzelle would pick someone else soon or the effect would be quite spoiled.

Luckily, Mamzelle's bones were not as tolerant of Beryl's weak French as usual, and, after correcting a few points impatiently, she pointed at Agnes, then Daisy-May and, finally, Millicent from Miss Sparks' house.

Millicent proceeded to read, she was quite a little actor and attempted to inject a wealth of feeling into each sentence, throwing out her arms theatrically, whilst keeping a marvellously straight face.

Mamzelle was not sure whether the girl was serious or not and was about to let someone else take over when Millicent reached the first cue.

Il y eut une rafale de vent glaciale et la fenêtre se referma avec un coup de coeur arretant.

The window of the first form classroom which had been at half-mast slammed down with a loud bang that almost brought Nan's heart to a stop- and she had been expecting it.

Mamzelle Meuhourat's eyes widened, and she clapped a hand to her heart, letting out a little shriek. A few of the girls squealed.

'C'est bon,' observed Mamzelle bravely, 'the window-she is shut now, she cannot frighten us again. It is the fault of these English mistresses. To have the window open on such a day as this it is madness, truly. Poppy, let us continue.'

Poppy went red and began in painfully slow French to follow the lines with her finger:

Tout fut tranquille. Soudain il y eut un terrible gémissement de la cheminée et une pluie de suie jaillit.

Leonora jerked on the string lying inconspicuously in her right hand and heard the tiny pop as the cork disengaged itself from the balloon. All of a sudden, the classroom was filled with the tortuous high-pitched moaning of a balloon emptying. It really was most realistic and several of the girls cried out. A large puff of soot descended from the chimney, hovering for a while as a cloud before settling as a black powder over the hearth and surrounding floorboards. Several of the girls nearest pulled their chairs away, coughing and spluttering as the fine particles of soot lodged in their throats.

This time the French mistress leapt to her feet and emitted a shrill scream, evidently very much affected, 'Nom d'un nom d'un nom! Qu'est ce qui se passe? On se trouve dans une école hantée. Ce n'est pas joli, ca!'

'Well, it's hardly surprising since we're so close to the ruins of Hillesley Castle,' opined Millicent, 'That's haunted, you know, by a Tudor lady who was murdered by her lover back in the fifteen hundreds. Legend has it she walks the grounds once a month trying to find him to have her revenge!'

Sarah screamed and Mamzelle turned white. 'You think then that this Tudor lady has come into my classroom?' she asked gravely, making Poppy snort violently.

'I think it's a possibility,' answered Millicent, equally serious.

'Then I go at once to Miss Montagu!' stormed Mamzelle dramatically, 'I will not share my classroom with ghosts!'

Barbara and Leonora shared alarmed glances; they didn't want Mamzelle to go to Miss Montagu with tales of being haunted.

Hastily, Leonora attempted to reassure the mistress, 'It's certainly a remarkable coincidence, Mamzelle. But, you know, that chimney is very dirty-'

Barbara smiled knowingly; she could testify as to that.

'-it probably hasn't been swept for a couple of years. It's only natural for it to shed a bit of soot.'

'Tu as raison,' conceded Mamzelle, calming down a bit, 'Ah, but the noise!' she added wildly, 'the terrible wailing!'

'Ah, yes, well that is harder to explain,' admitted Leonora, her brow creased in thought.

'It could be a bird,' suggested Wang Li unexpectedly, anxious for a piece of the action, 'It could be a bird who has fallen in there and is stuck!'

'Ah, le pauvre!' moaned Mamzelle softly, her compassion stirred.

'It's a mighty strange bird if so,' whispered Barbara, permitting herself a grin.

Just as Mamzelle was approaching the chimney tentatively in order to try and find the poor trapped bird, the door opened, and Miss Porter appeared looking somewhat annoyed that it had not been opened for her as was usual.

Her annoyance turned to amazement on seeing Mamzelle peering up the chimney, an expression of deep concern on her face.

Unaware of the first from mistress' presence, Mamzelle began whistling softly, making little encouraging sounds to the non-existent bird. This was just too much for Elaine, who burst out into a guffaw that died on her lips as she met Miss Porter's icy glare. The first formers' eyes swung from one mistress to the other. They desperately wanted to laugh but the look on their form mistress' face subdued them.

Coughing slightly at the coal dust that still hung in the air, Miss Porter addressed Mamzelle's large back, 'Mamzelle Meuhourat, what on Earth is the matter? It's three o'clock. Surely you take the fourth form now.'

On hearing her colleague's voice, Mamzelle had almost jumped out of her skin. Now, she looked at the clock on the wall behind the teacher's desk and saw to her dismay that it was indeed three o'clock.

Frowning, she consulted her watch, gasped, gave it

a remonstrative tap, and exclaimed, 'Oh, la, la, my watch she has stopped.'

'Well, you can't have remembered to wind it up,' said Miss Porter shortly, not about to be thrown off course discussing the time, 'I do not understand what is going on here? What are you looking for up the chimney? And how come there is such a lot of soot on the floor?'

'Ah!' seemingly aware for the first time of the small mountain of soot on which she was standing, Mamzelle retreated hastily, brushing at her shear stockings with a delicate lace handkerchief, 'There is a bird who is stuck up there,' she explained, then added incoherently, 'But when I first heard your voice, I thought you were the ghost.'

'*The* ghost?' queried Miss Porter, 'why should I be a ghost?' The mistress' eyes flicked to where Leonora and Barbara were sitting, trying and failing to appear uninterested in the bizarre exchange.

'The school, it is haunted!' proclaimed Mamzelle dramatically and nodded her head several times as though this somehow lent credence to the statement.

'And what has given you that idea?' asked Miss Porter, going straight to the nub of the issue.

'Oh, Mademoiselle Porter, if you knew the agonies we have suffered, n'est-ce pas, mes filles?'

No one answered. Miss Porter looked suspiciously around at the silent eyes that refused to meet her own.

Beryl gave the French mistress a faint smile, wishing she would be quiet.

'First the window, it comes crashing down with such a noise. All by its own. Then, ah, then the fireplace it begins to scream. The wailing- it was truly not from a voice of this world!'

Miss Porter, much to Mamzelle's annoyance, appeared to have stopped listening. She had gone to the fireplace where her sharp eyes had caught a gleam of pink rubber amongst the soot.

Stooping, she extracted the sorry remains of the rubber balloon and handed them to Mamzelle before wiping her hands clean on her handkerchief. 'Your ghost, Mamzelle.'

Mamzelle stared down at the late balloon in her large hand and the truth dawned on her. It was just a trick. The bad girls were having their Mamzelle on. Staring around at their now terrified faces, Mamzelle thought how she had just unwittingly let the cat out of the bag for them and emitted a snort of laughter.

Miss Porter, meanwhile, was bearing down on the two culprits, 'Leonora Jameson, I believe I told you you were to sit on the front row during lessons. Come on now everyone and get your books out. This is my lesson time we are wasting,' she added with a pointed glance at her wristwatch.

'Aha,' said the mistress grimly, 'We have our culprit.'

Leonora squirmed; she had meant to change places before the geography lesson. She got up and opened her desk a crack to get the books out, aware that the evidence of the trick was inside.

Miss Porter, seeing her reluctance, promptly forced up the desk lid, her gaze falling at once on the small clump of once invisible string, now coated in soot, one end still attached to the cork. 'Aha!' said the mistress grimly, 'we have our culprit.'

Barbara, unable to watch Leonora be found guilty alone, stammered out a confession. Wang Li added her voice, and Nan and Poppy and one or two others piped up as well.

'Well,' said their form mistress coldly, 'since you all seem so eager to be punished you can all donate your Saturday morning to cleaning up this appalling mess. And you can all come to me after prep. tonight to catch up the quarter of an hour of this lesson that you have wasted.'

There were groans at this, but Miss Porter hadn't finished, 'as for the two ringleaders of this charade, I'm sure that Mamzelle Meuhourat will be only too pleased to give you some extra coaching in French.'

Mamzelle's face lit up at this, 'Ah, yes, these damp weekends. But we shall not mind, we will study la belle langue française toute l'après-midi.'

'A fine sentiment Mamzelle, but perhaps you ought

to be leaving us to our geography now. The fourth form are no doubt wondering where you've got to.'

Mamzelle's eyes widened in alarm as she remembered the time and she fairly galloped out of the room, leaving a deflated first form to slog at their geography under Miss Porter's unrelenting eye.

~ 16 ~

Two Pieces of good News

That weekend the feelings of the first formers were very mixed. Elaine was elated and simply couldn't stop reminiscing about the 'capital trick!' Leonora showed herself annoyed, but Nan knew that she was in fact relishing the praise.

Barbara and Leonora were hardly to be seen the whole of Saturday as Mamzelle Meuhourat, under the impression that they too were enjoying themselves, kept them in for most of the day.

'I never knew French verbs could be so painful,' complained Leonora, as soon as Mamzelle had left the room for five minutes.

'That's because you've never had to work hard before,' said Barbara, a trifle jealously, 'you just seem to get good grades without making an effort.'

'Well, I'm making an effort now all right,' grumbled Leonora, 'I shouldn't be surprised to see French verbs coming out of my ears.'

'Well, I'll keep a look-out,' promised Barbara sardonically. 'I'm getting up to stretch my legs a bit.' She jumped up and performed a series of Swedish exercises rapidly, before scrambling back on her chair as Mamzelle re-entered. The two first formers brightened. She bore a tray laden with three mugs of steaming hot cocoa, 'Shh, it is our little secret,' she whispered, as she retook her place and continued briskly, 'who can tell me the verbs that take être?'

Nan, meanwhile, was filled with anticipation for she was to find out if she had made the Lacrosse team.

Early on the Sunday morning she was up and on the Lacrosse field. It was a gorgeous autumnal morning. The sun, a warm golden disc, was still low in the sky, filtering through the translucent leaves that glistened like so many jewels. Red, orange, yellow, green and all colours in between. The sunlight fell in linear rays at Nan's feet, like feelers putting out to thaw the frosty dew that crunched under Nan's sturdy boots.

The other Lower School girls hopeful of making the team trickled gradually onto the pitch and stood around, their breath forming little clouds of mist in the cold air.

Two Pieces of good News

At last Amrita and the team captain from the third form, who had already been chosen, turned up. The third former was big and bouncy with dark hair and an open likeable face.

'Right, gather round everyone,' called Amrita in a business-like voice, 'I'm sorry I've kept you all waiting but you're all so good that Heather and I wanted to make sure that we'd picked the best team.'

There were twenty of them not including the sixth former. That meant that eight of them would be disappointed. The only other first former there was Millicent from Miss Sparks' house. The others were all second and third formers. Although she desperately wanted to make the team, Nan understood that, as first formers, she and Millicent might not get to play this year, but they still might make the reserves.

Amrita had begun reading out the names of the lucky girls. At each name, Nan lost a little more hope, until finally there was only one position left to fill. It was too much to hope, she hadn't made it.

'Nan Miller,' ended Amrita and gave her a proud smile.

Nan's eyes widened in stunned surprise and her face broke into an ecstatic grin. She hardly dared believe it.

'First reserve- Millicent Appleby,' went on Amrita and Millicent's eyes almost fell out of head, 'Congratulations,' smiled the Games Captain warmly.

Porcine Pranks at St. Anne's

A few of the disappointed older girls were muttering disgustedly and sending hostile looks in her direction but Nan hardly noticed. She couldn't wait to write and tell her parents.

'Right,' continued Amrita briskly, 'now that we have our team, I think we ought to put in some practice. We'll just use half the field, and the attackers and defenders can practice going against one another.'

Nan wore herself out setting up goals for Lucie, an ambitious and rather bumptious second former, but Heather, who played in goal, was simply too good and not many got past her. Nan got herself into some good positions to be able to score herself, but no one would pass to her.

On a few occasions, Amrita stepped in, and Nan was allowed a shot on goal, but she was always so aware of the expectant, slightly threatening stares of the others that she kept fumbling the throw. Frustration rose up in her- if her own teammates were so reluctant to let her play how would she fare against their opponents? Nan pushed down these thoughts, however. After all if she could help Lucie to score a goal then that was her job done and anyway, she reminded herself, she was just thrilled to have made the team at all.

On entering the common room later that morning, Nan found everyone huddled together around Barbara in the middle of the room, whispering furiously. On hearing her enter, though, they all surged around eagerly to hear her news.

'How was it?'

'Did you make the team?'

'What happened?'

Nan told them happily and there were gasps of admiration.

'Well done old thing!' cried Poppy grinning and looking almost as pleased as Nan as she squeezed her arm.

'Yes, jolly good show!' added Beryl, clapping her on the back, 'it takes an exceptional first former to make the team.'

'And Millicent is first reserve,' added Nan, wishing as she said it that Millicent could have made the team too.

'Is she?' queried Barbara, a strange expression on her face, 'what a pity she didn't quite make it; you two work so well as a team.'

Nan's surprise must have shown on her face for Barbara continued, 'I've watched a few of your practice sessions from the top lawn. You were so focused I'm not surprised that you didn't spot me. Oh, well, at least if one of the team drop out Millicent will be able to take their place.'

'Well, don't let's wish illness on any of the second formers,' said Daisy-May briskly, 'I'm sure that you'll

Porcine Pranks at St. Anne's

make a fine team. After all, Amrita's a fine Games Captain and she picked you all.'

Seeing the truth of this, Nan tried to banish all doubts from her mind. Presently, though, she was so diverted that all thoughts of Lacrosse vanished.

'Anyway,' Beryl was continuing, 'you didn't hear what we were all talking about just before you came in.'

'We're going to have a midnight feast,' explained Barbara, her eyes sparkling, 'It's my birthday in three weeks' time on the eighth of December and it will be a Saturday. My Aunt has given me half a crown so I'm going to choose something special for the feast.'

'We'll all bring something along too,' said Poppy, 'My Aunt gave me sixpence at half-term, and I haven't spent it yet.'

'Ooh,' cried Elaine excitedly, 'I can hardly wait.' Everyone smiled at her, amused. It was hard to remember that she was the same person as the morose, withdrawn girl that they had known at the start of term. 'I say, Poppy, can Bobby come?'

'Can Bobby eat chocolate?' Beryl wanted to know.

'Well, yes, it doesn't do her any harm,' answered Poppy slowly, 'But Elaine, I don't really think we can smuggle her up to the dormitory in the dead of night- it's to risky. And, besides, she's grown awfully; I couldn't carry her.'

Two Pieces of good News

'Oh,' Elaine's face fell. Since promising to look after Bobby she had been as good as her word and a real bond had sprung up between the two. 'Well couldn't we at least save her something from the feast and give it to her the next day?'

'Yes, we could easily do that,' agreed Poppy readily.

'Absolutely,' said Barbara, 'we all love Bobby, and she deserves a treat. She's been existing on kitchen scraps for weeks.'

'Yes, but they're very high-quality kitchen scraps,' put in Elaine seriously, making everyone laugh.

17

Leonora on the Case

As the days grew shorter and it started getting dark at four o'clock there was less time to spend outside, and everyone clustered around the common room fire for warmth. Nan took up Barbara's offer and borrowed a P.G. Wodehouse book off her.

'Where's *Something Fresh*?' asked Nan from her bed where she sat swinging her stockinged feet.

'Oh, I don't know if I've still got that one here,' said Barbara, her voice muffled as she burrowed deeper and deeper into the depths of her bedside cabinet. 'I swap them over at half-term. Oh, no, you're in luck, here it is,' so-saying she fished out the well-thumbed copy and handed it to Nan.

'Thank you,' said Nan and was soon deeply immersed

in it. She found herself laughing out loud. So much so that Poppy came over to see what was so funny and began reading over Nan's shoulder.

Wang Li spent more time in the little music rooms near the hall, practicing her piano, and the first formers would stop to listen whenever they were passing for Wang Li really had improved marvellously.

One day, Leonora was on her way to Mamzelle's study to hand in a French essay on 'Ce que j'ai fait pendant les vacances d'été' which as its title suggests was due in the first week of term but whose absence the French mistress had only just noticed. The melodious notes of the piano came to her ears and she was just thinking how well she would like to play if only she had the patience when the tune came to an abrupt halt to be replaced by a series of deep booming thumps on the keys.

Curious, Leonora gently opened the door and saw Wang Li slumped on the piano stool, her head resting on the instrument, jet black hair spread out over the ivory keys.

'Wang Li!' cried Leonora aghast and slightly embarrassed for emotions were not the girl's strong point.

Wang Li's head shot up and Leonora saw that her eyes were red from crying.

Wang Li's head shot up and Leonora saw that her eyes were red from crying.

'I say, whatever is the matter?' asked her classmate, shutting the door and pulling up a chair. Leonora's natural role was not that of comforter, but she did her best, patting the girl awkwardly on the back and offering a somewhat crumpled handkerchief.

'Thank you,' sniffed Wang Li substituting it for her own and wiping her face.

'Sorry,' grinned Leonora in an attempt to cheer her friend up, 'I'm not sure how long that's been in my pocket for; you're probably wise not to use it.'

Wang Li smiled back and after a few moments to steady her voice, explained, 'It's nothing really, I mean, it's not worth getting upset about, but it's so relentless.'

Leonora looked a question.

'Miss Winter's bullying. I know she bullies everyone, but I think she really must hate me. Nothing I can do is ever right. That's why I have to practice so hard. Because if I make even the smallest mistake in lessons, she comes down on me like a... a bag of bricks.'

'Tonne,' corrected Leonora absently, her forehead creased in thought.

'I sometimes think that I should write to Mama and Baba and tell them that I do not want any more piano lessons, but then she would have got what she wanted,' Wang Li's chin shot up in determination, 'And I will not let her get the better of me.'

'Well, personally, I can't see how you can cram so

much into your brain,' admitted Leonora, scratching her head, 'but you seem to manage it and it seems a shame that your piano lessons aren't more enjoyable. What you need is a different teacher.' A glint came into the first former's eyes, 'I bet Miss Montagu wouldn't want Miss Winter to teach at St. Anne's anymore if she knew what she was really like. The school would really be much better off without bad eggs like her cluttering it up.'

'You mean,' said Wang Li, groping, 'that we should tell Miss Montagu?'

'No,' said Leonora shocked, 'that would be boring. No, you leave this to me. I have the glimmer of a plan.'

The Chinese girl shot her a questioning look. Answering the question with another, Leonora mused, 'Beryl Forsyth takes piano lessons too, doesn't she? But Miss Winter doesn't bully *her*?'

'Oh, no, everybody loves Beryl,' returned Wang Li, a slight note of bitterness detectable in her tone.

'Umm,' said Leonora thoughtfully, 'you leave this with me, Wang Li, old girl. I think I've hit on a way to make Miss Winter disappear.'

And with a nod and a wink, Leonora herself disappeared leaving Wang Li wondering what on Earth she had in mind for the troublesome drama mistress.

∽ 18 ∾

A Lacrosse Match

Nan, meanwhile, was very busy over the next couple of weeks. The inter-school lacrosse tournament had begun, and she had played in every match so far. There were three other schools taking part- Miss Lindsey's School for Girls, St Catherine's and Miss Martineau's School for Young Ladies. Each school played the others twice- once at home and once away- making six matches in all. St Anne's had won their first match, drawn the next two and lost the last one. Now there were just the two matches against Miss Martineau's remaining.

Nan was feeling depressed with her team's performance. She knew that they could quite easily have won all their matches had they pulled together as a proper team, but they had not. Out on the pitch, Nan found acres of space and yelled herself hoarse calling for the ball but not one of the attackers would pass to her. She managed a few tackles and from these set up a few goals, but the others never returned the favour, preferring to shoot for goal themselves no matter how far away or closely marked they were. The whole thing was making Nan sick. What was the point of giving of her best when her own team were so beastly towards her? And why were they? It couldn't be merely because she was the only first former on the team, surely? First formers had made the team before. Nan could think of nothing she had done to make them resent her and so was forced to the conclusion that the sole reason was the shade of her skin.

This conclusion made Nan feel very down and depressed indeed, but she was not going to let them get to her. She would show them how good she was at lacrosse. It was just so difficult when one was all alone. Heather, the team captain, had noticed that poor Nan was never passed to and, to her credit, had remonstrated with Lucie and her second form cronies on the subject, but from her position in goal there was little she could do to influence play on the field. Amrita also noticed from where she stood watching at the sidelines and yelled at the second formers to pass but there was not much she could do either. Nan thought that she was regretting having put Lucie on the team, but Lucie was a very good player so did not see how she could very well take her out.

This problem was solved the day before the home match by Lucie herself. Caught up in a crush of girls all thudding down the back stairs, she tripped and broke her ankle to the immense delight of the first formers.

'So, you will be able to play after all, Millicent,' observed Barbara, clapping the girl heartily on the back.

Millicent gave her lopsided sarcastic grin, 'Yes, what luck! Or was it? You know, I wouldn't put it past Leonora to have given our dear Lucie a well-timed shove.'

'As if I'd do a thing like that to any of my fellow human beings!' cried Leonora in exaggerated outrage but there was a twinkle in her eye and Nan wondered if there could possibly be any truth in Millicent's accusation. But, no, Leonora may be fond of a trick and a joke now and again, but Nan could not believe her capable of deliberate violence.

The day of the match arrived, and the morning seemed to creep by as though on tip toe. Nan was horribly on edge and could hardly eat anything at dinner. At last their opponents drew up on the crunching gravel drive in their supercilious coaches. They descended to form a neat row like neat pins and Nan gasped as she got her first glimpse of them for at first sight, they all appeared curiously identical. All were blond and blue-eyed and doll-like. This effect was emphasised by their Lacrosse uniforms. They wore very feminine pleated blouse like dresses and matching, coloured neckties all finished with elaborate gold brooches. Their golden hair was all permed on top of their heads in the grown-up fashion that would not have been permitted at St. Anne's.

'Golly, where do they suppose they are?' whispered Poppy into Nan's ear and she giggled. The Miss Martineau's girls really did look quite ludicrous, and Nan would have laughed had she not felt so daunted by their blondness.

The St. Anne's Lacrosse team all looked very smart indeed in their plain knee-length sports dresses, study boots and hair tied neatly back.

Miss Knight looked very young and sporty indeed stood next to the games mistress from Miss Martineau's school who was so very drab and severe looking that Nan wondered how on Earth she could teach sport. As for their team captain, she was a haughty looking specimen whose fine features might have been attractive had they not been continually contorted into a look of intense contempt.

Things did not get off to a very good start. The first thing to happen was that Nan was barred from stepping on to the pitch by the Miss Martineau's games mistress.

'Only members of the Lacrosse teams allowed on the pitch,' she stated menacingly, blocking Nan's way.

'I am a member of the St. Anne's Lacrosse team,' an infuriated Nan forced herself to reply through clenched teeth, fuming at the impudence of the woman.

'Nan is a team member,' echoed Millicent, coming up to stand beside her friend and staring the games mistress down with a frostiness of glare worthy of Miss Porter.

The woman closed her mouth with a snap, narrowed her eyes and looked about to argue the point further when Miss Knight appeared all smiles to usher the two first formers over to the rest of the team.

Without Lucie there to rally them they looked a bedraggled bunch, but they also smiled at the two first formers giving Nan the hope that without the second former's malevolent influence they might just show the team spirit needed to win the match.

Eying their opponents, Nan felt a knot of angst tighten in her stomach, their smug looks serving to intimidate her.

Presently, Miss Knight blew her whistle and the gentle murmur of chatter ceased. A few words were said, the two captains shook hands rather grimly and the players took up their positions.

Another pip from the whistle and the two centres were scrabbling for the ball. The St. Anne's girl got it in her net and without further ado lobbed it to the girl to her right who ran with it a few metres before being tackled viciously and losing it to the other side.

Seeing the victor of the tackle running straight at her, Nan met her and locked sticks, dislodging the ball and catching it neatly in her net. Hardly able to believe her luck, Nan tore down the pitch, her boots slipping in the wet grass coated in crystals of frost.

Noticing that Millicent was unmarked, Nan stopped and sent the ball flying to her. Beaming her approval of Nan's throw, her teammate caught it deftly before sending it spinning for their opponents' goal. It eluded the goalkeeper and rolled between the posts. St Anne's were ahead.

Nan bounded back to her start place, feeling so giddy with joy that she felt she was walking on air. A great cheer broke out among the many watching St. Anne's students and Nan spied her classmates jumping up and down at the front of the crowd of spectators lining the edge of the field. Poppy gave her a thumbs up and she returned it quickly before once more finding herself in the thick of the game.

This time, however, the girls from Miss Martineau's knew who to look out for and marked Nan and Millicent relentlessly.

From being beside herself with joy Nan plummeted to desperation when Heather let a goal in making the score equal. Neatly dodging two of her opponents, she intercepted a pass and picked out an attentive second former. Hurling the ball at her, Nan prepared to follow the progress of the game when out of nowhere two girls from Miss Martineau's barged into her, knocking her roughly to the ground. Startled, Nan easily lost her balance and toppled over backwards, landing on the hard, sharply iced earth. Smirking maliciously, the two perpetrators ran on as though nothing had happened, leaving Nan to get unsteadily to her feet. The experience had shaken her, and looking hopefully at her teammates, the spectators and Miss Knight and being unable to meet the eye of any of them, Nan's unease deepened as she realised that no one had witnessed the incident. Miss Knight's eyes were glued to the ball and, as Nan hadn't even had the ball when she was attacked there was little chance that she had seen anything. Indeed, if she had, she would surely have stopped the match.

Trying to calm her pounding heart, Nan took several long, deep breaths. It was a good job she had so much adrenaline flooding through her body, or her legs would have been shaking. She was very glad indeed when the whistle was blown for half-time, and everyone streamed off the pitch to receive their orange segments.

Sucking at her orange segment despondently, Nan stuck close to Millicent, trying to find the words to tell her what had occurred. Millicent was grim and drawn, however, and disinclined to conversation, as she always was in the middle of an important match. The air was so noisy anyway with the excited chatter and cries and taunts of the two teams and their spectators that Nan could hardly hear herself above the roar.

Nan returned to the pitch determined to win the match.

Only two minutes into the second half, however, Miss Martineau's team scored another goal, now leading two to one. The St. Anne's team would have to score two goals to win whilst preventing their opponents from getting any more.

Realising that she was getting the worst of the marking on their team, Nan dodged about, drawing their opponents away from the St. Anne's players. This was quite a risky strategy, as the Miss Martineau's girls had shown that they were not above using violence, but Nan was nimble on her feet and kept just out of reach.

This strategy eventually led to one of the second formers being able to score and the scales were balanced once more.

Worn out from all her skipping about, Nan was relieved to find that her opponents now avoided her, having cottoned on to her trick. This was exactly what Nan had been wishing for, for now she could find acres of space. Keeping cool and focused on the game,

A Lacrosse Match

Nan positioned herself at the far end of the field with Millicent a few feet away and waited on their teammates progress up the pitch.

It was a textbook goal. Kathy, one of the third formers on the team, evaded several opponents, keeping the ball securely in her net. Then, cornered and about to be tackled, she flung the stick up over her head and the ball flew through the air above her opponents' heads to Millicent who was awaiting it. Making the most of a short window of opportunity, Millicent passed the ball to Nan who was only a few feet from the goal.

Feeling the weight of the ball straining the net at the end of her Lacrosse stick, Nan half turned, brought the stick back onto her shoulder before jerking it upwards. The ball shot out and sped straight into the back of the goal.

Nan's face broke into an ecstatic grin and the St. Anne's supporters erupted into wild cheers. Disappointment and disgust were etched into the unsmiling faces of the young ladies from Miss Martineau's school as the whistle signalled the end of the match. Nan was quite astonished; she had not realised there was so little time left. She had only just scored in time.

Spotting Poppy and Barbara waving frantically, Nan longed to join them, but first the players had to shake hands to show that there was no ill feeling between the two sides. It was a gesture that the girls from Miss

The ball shot out and sped straight into the back of the goal.

A Lacrosse Match

Martineau's seemed reluctant to perform and only did so with very bad grace.

They shook hands with Nan in a somewhat grudging manner and Nan could have assured them that the feeling was quite mutual. The last two did not shake Nan's hand at all but merely stood sniggering, leaving her hand outstretched. Recognising them as the two bullies who had pushed her over, Nan snatched her hand back, glad that they had not sullied it and shoved them to the back of her mind decisively, racing over to join Poppy.

19

An Unpleasant Encounter

'I say, you were absolutely wizard Nan!' praised Poppy warmly as the first formers tucked into the special tea in the hall laid on for the benefit of the two Lacrosse teams. The tables were filled with all kinds of treats. Sausage rolls, plates of cold meats, bread and butter, dishes of tinned fruit, big dark fruit cakes, bowls of thick yellow custard all washed down with thirst-quenching lemonade. Nan found that she was quite ravenous after all her running about in the frosty air and even those girls who had only been spectators to the match seemed to be doing themselves well.

'Yes,' added Beryl, licking a thoughtful spoon clean of custard, 'you scored the winning goal! I bet there's not many first formers done that.

An Unpleasant Encounter

'And Millicent scored first,' Leonora reminded them, clapping the two on the back, 'That's two goals scored by first formers!'

'Well, Nan and Millicent were the best two players on the pitch,' enthused Barbara, 'I always said that you and Millicent made a splendid team.'

Nan looked around at her friends and beamed with pride and pleasure. How nice it was to be surrounded by such good friends and how wonderful to have helped win such an important match. She couldn't wait to write and tell her parents; wouldn't they be proud of her. Nan hugged herself, all her previous anxiety forgotten.

After she had eaten her fill of the glorious tea, Nan suddenly longed to be somewhere quieter. The hall was full to bursting with laughing chattering girls and Nan's senses began to feel a little overwhelmed. Her face and hands felt hot and clammy with the dramatic change of temperature from the icy conditions outside to the stifling heat of the crowded hall. So, murmuring her intention to Poppy, Nan slid off her chair and made her way to the changing rooms to get out of her muddy games kit.

This she did and she was just drying off her face, having washed it at the basin when she heard the door open and saw the reflexions of four girls in the mirror. But they were not St. Anne's girls. They were from Miss Martineau's school.

A cold hand of terror closed over Nan's heart as she recognised the two bullies from earlier now accompanied by two of their cronies and obviously out for her blood.

There was no mistaking the self-satisfied smirks on their hate-filled faces. A wild panic gripped Nan and she turned quickly and made for the door. But the four girls closed ranks cutting off her escape.

'Going somewhere?' inquired bully number one sneeringly and Nan felt the colour drain from her face as she felt suddenly faint. All she could do was stand there, rooted to the spot, her heart pounding in her ears and her legs pulsing as if they had turned suddenly to hot liquid jelly. Why, oh, why, had she not brought Poppy with her?

She knew the answer. She had thought she was safe. She had never dreamed that anything like this could happen at St. Anne's.

And what was happening, thought Nan, as one of her tormentors took a step towards her. Above the sensations of terror, Nan was conscious of a sense of utter shock and disbelief. That these total strangers, whose names she didn't know and who did not know hers, could feel so incensed by her presence as to seek her out with she dare not think what intentions was incomprehensible and wildly alarming.

'Go home!' snarled the leader of the little group as

An Unpleasant Encounter

Nan took a step backwards. Go home? What did she mean? Nan had only ever lived in England. Could it be that she didn't really belong? A wave of emotion swept over her and Nan fought desperately against it, trying to look the girl confidently in the eye even as she was assailed by sudden painful doubts. Nan stared at her assailants uncomprehendingly, unable to reply for a hot glue sticking her mouth together.

'Go back to your own country!' jeered another, stepping up to Nan and pushing her roughly. The girl found herself careering into one of the laughing bullies, who promptly shoved her away. Soon Nan was being pushed from one girl to another, her vision blurred and her head throbbing with dizziness. She was aware of insults and laughter directed at her, but she heard it as though it was coming from a long way away or she was underwater. She could not focus on one particular thing; it was like a horrible nightmare filled with hateful jeering faces.

Worn out from physical exertion and dizzy with mental torment, a wave of nausea hit Nan and she felt physically sick. Someone grabbed her arms and held them behind her, and things looked to be getting grim when suddenly the door flew open and a familiar voice said in a clear and dangerously level voice, 'What's going on in here?'

It was Wang Li!

Porcine Pranks at St. Anne's

Nan's heart leapt or it would have done if she were not so exhausted.

Momentarily distracted from Nan, the Miss Martineau's girls crowed over the fresh prey that had wandered their way, letting Nan slither to the floor unnoticed.

One of the girls who had pushed Nan made her eyes into slits and jabbered in a sickening impression of Chinese sounds. Wang Li paled but advanced boldly into the room and only Nan felt the tremor in her hand as she took hers and helped her to her feet.

Having rescued Nan, Wang Li would have made an unobtrusive exit, but the bullies had other plans.

'Where do you think you're going?' cried a voice and a fist slammed out of nowhere for Nan's face.

Coolly master of the situation, Wang Li nudged Nan aside, grabbed hold of the fist and yanked it forwards, neatly dodging away as the girl on the other end of it overbalanced and was sent spinning to the floor, carried on by her own momentum.

Before Nan had time to recover from the shock of seeing Wang Li's martial arts skills in action, they were called upon again.

The girl who had taunted Wang Li now made to slap her across the face, but Wang Li caught hold of her wrist, twisting her arm into a lock and making the sufferer cry out in pain before regretfully relinquishing

An Unpleasant Encounter

her. She fell to her knees, clutching her arm as the third girl advanced on Nan. Almost before Nan had time to feel afraid, Wang Li had felled her, sweeping her legs from under her so that she landed in an undignified heap on the bathroom floor.

Defeated, the three bullies made a hasty exit, sobbing over their various injuries and joined by the fourth girl who wisely decided not to cross Wang Li.

As the door swung shut on the cowards, Nan stared at her friend in awe. She didn't know why she was so surprised; she had witnessed the girl's kung fu skills in training after all. But this was the first time that she had seen them in action, and, she prayed, the last.

Wang Li was already striding purposefully towards the door, and Nan followed quickly, glad to leave the scene of so much trauma behind. Her legs felt clunky as she walked and she felt light-headed and faint, her heart still fluttering unpleasantly. She wondered how Wang Li felt and if she had derived any pleasure from her small victories. She had a small smile on her lips, but it was grim rather than triumphant.

Only when they reached the comparative safety of the empty first form classroom did a word pass between the two girls.

'I say,' said Nan, still breathless from her ordeal, 'Thanks awfully for rescuing me; I daren't think what might have happened if you hadn't turned up when you did.' She said this lightly because the thought was too dreadful to contemplate.

Without answering, Wang Li got up from the desk she had been sitting on and flung her arms around Nan. Nan, quite overcome, felt strengthened by her warm touch and hugged her back, her tears making the shoulder of Wang Li's blazer sodden.

'Bù kè qì, you're welcome,' said Wang Li, her voice muffled, 'I think perhaps it would be a good idea if I taught you some defensive moves.'

'Thank you,' said Nan shakily, her teeth chattering from the anxiety, 'Will you come with me?'

'Of course,' answered Wang Li promptly, taking Nan's hand protectively in her own. There was no need for the Chinese girl to ask Nan where she was going. They turned their steps in the direction of Miss Montagu's study and were soon standing outside on the landing.

The headmistress' clear voice bade them enter and they did so, closing the door softly behind them.

Nan was surprised to see Amrita sat in the chair opposite the Head, and was afraid of intruding, but Miss Montagu, seeing their ashen faces, sprang to her feet and drew up two extra chairs for them.

'I say, Nan!' exclaimed Amrita, getting up to shake the first former's hand warmly, 'That was an absolutely

An Unpleasant Encounter

marvellous goal. You should be very proud of yourself.'

'Are you all right, Nan?' asked Miss Montagu gently.

Nan felt a lump constricting her throat at the question and could only shake her head.

'Take a seat,' ordered the headmistress firmly and the two girls sank thankfully onto the cushioned chairs, 'Now, you both look like you could do with a hot mug of cocoa. Wait there whilst I just ask for some.'

Miss Montagu pulled an old-fashioned bell-pull next to the fireplace, and in an amazingly short space of time a neatly dressed maid in black dress and frothy white lace apron and cap was at the door.

'Four large mugs of cocoa please Mary,' said Miss Montagu crisply.

'Yes, ma'am,' said Mary and disappeared.

The headmistress of St. Anne's would not let either Nan or Wang Li say a word until Mary had returned with her silver tray.

'I've brought shortbread as well, ma'am,' she confessed righteously. She was a funny prim little thing with a cockney accent that fitted ill with her posh air.

'Thank you, Mary.'

Mary withdrew and Miss Montagu handed Nan and Wang Li their steaming mugs. Nan took a tentative sip, but it was just the right temperature. The warm sugary mixture flooded her body and she felt herself feeling better with every sip.

'Now then,' said the headmistress, seeing the colour return to their cheeks, 'What has happened to upset you?'

Nan told her quickly and succinctly what had occurred, 'I went to get changed and four girls from Miss Martineau's followed me there and started insulting me and then they were pushing me about, and-'

'They were about to hit Nan when I arrived,' put in Wang Li, 'then they bullied me also and tried to hurt us both but I-'

'Wang Li showed them some of her kung fu moves,' finished Nan managing to smile for the first time.

Miss Montagu did not smile. Nan had never seen her look so grim before. Her hand clenched on her desk, and she swiped it hastily off, 'That such a thing could happen in my school,' she breathed, and her voice was barely controlled. 'Nan are you much hurt?' she added in more normal tones.

'Umm,' Nan looked down at herself doubtfully and rubbed her arm, 'just a bit bruised, I think. Wang Li came just in time.'

And Thank Goodness you did, Wang Li,' said the headmistress in heartfelt tones, 'you have both shown incredible bravery today,' she smiled at them suddenly, 'I am very proud of both of you. Not just for how you acted in the face of this despicable bullying but for having the courage to come to me about it.'

An Unpleasant Encounter

Nan looked at the kind, calm, good woman in front of her and felt unutterably glad that she was the headmistress of St. Anne's.

'Unfortunately,' continued Miss Montagu and again there was that barely concealed anger in her voice, 'I can do very little in the way of punishing the individuals involved. I shall telephone Miss Martineau and report this incident to her, but I have very little hope of her punishing her students. I'm afraid her school is very different from my own. It has only been open a year, so I have not had much chance of observing her methods first-hand, but what I have heard I have not liked, and this incident proves my worst fears. Of course, if the girls were further up the school, I would involve the police, but I do not wish to do so with such young children. However, what I can do I will, and you may rest assured that St. Anne's will never play another match against Miss Martineau's-'

Miss Montagu broke off as a gurgling sound came from Amrita and she choked in the act of drinking her cocoa. Nan was breathing a sigh of profound relief. She had felt sick to the bottom of her stomach at the thought of playing another match against Miss Martineau's, but she had not wanted to let the team down. She had to be so much braver than most of her peers though, and she did not want to be brave; she just wanted to be normal. At Miss Montagu's words a huge weight rolled off her shoulders as she realised the Head understood.

Porcine Pranks at St. Anne's

Amrita, however, was staring at the headmistress in consternation. 'But Miss Montagu!' she exclaimed croakily, 'You can't do that! We simply must play this last match! It's the very last one and if we win it, we win the tournament!'

The headmistress held up a hand and the games captain froze. 'I'm surprised at you Amrita,' said Miss Montagu rather sharply, 'surely you see that I cannot possibly put my students in danger. Nan will not play in that match, and I certainly do not want her to feel any pressure to do so.'

Amrita made a sound like a dying duck and hastened to explain herself, 'Of course Nan cannot possibly be expected to play, but mightn't I at least ask the others? The honour of the school is at stake!'

Miss Montagu sighed heavily, 'Amrita, I don't care tuppence for the honour of the school. What I do care about is the safety of the girls in my care.'

Nan and Wang Li exchanged bemused glances. It was funny to hear a headmistress talk so scathingly of her school's honour when so many schools seemed to live for nothing else but their peculiar traditions and own distorted sense of right. Miss Montagu's no-nonsense attitude was refreshing and, Nan felt sadly, a rarity. At that moment she felt an enormous pride in St. Anne's and was heartily glad that her parents had sent her there and not to any other school. Why, she

An Unpleasant Encounter

might have gone to Miss Martineau's; horrid thought!

'But, Miss Montagu,' Amrita was pleading, 'We simply must win this match! Just this one match and then we need never play Miss Martineau's again. *Please*!'

'You games captains are all alike,' grumbled Miss Montagu, but she was wavering. 'Very well,' she said at last, 'you may send a team with Miss Knight, but Nan stays here, *and*,' she said emphatically, 'So do you.'

'But-' began Amrita alarmed.

'That is an order,' Miss Montagu informed her firmly, 'If Wang Li and Nan have been targeted today that means that anyone who looks a little different will not be safe. I would certainly not feel happy sending you off to their school.'

'But surely as games captain I would be safe,' ventured Amrita, but for the first time there was a note of doubt in her voice.

Nan couldn't see what Amrita wanted to go to Miss Martineau's for, but she supposed that as games captain she wanted to do what was expected of her and accompany the team.

Amrita was frowning, 'All right,' she said at last, 'I don't really want to go. I'll stay, but the team must go and win the match for us.'

Nan pulled a face as she thought of poor Millicent.

'That's settled then,' announced the headmistress brightly, and stood up, 'Well, I should think you'll be wanting to go and celebrate your win with the rest of your form,' she said kindly to Nan and Wang Li. 'Thank you for coming to see me; I'm only sorry I can't be more useful. The world is full of people we do not always see eye to eye with, but the majority of people are good, or so I seem to find. The haters are the minority; always remember that.'

'I can't understand them,' said Wang Li, speaking her mind for the first time, 'They frighten me,' she added, and Nan stared at her in surprise. Wang Li, who had so coolly disposed of the four bullies, had been frightened! It seemed incredible!

'Then you showed great bravery today. Both of you have shown great maturity, and I am sure that you both have the makings of brilliant Head Girls,' said Miss Montagu gravely, and Nan's heart thrilled with pride at such praise, 'but one shouldn't be frightened of bullies; they are really the most cowardly of creatures. And they come in all shapes and sizes too. Adults, can unfortunately be bullies just as easily as children can, and, in my experience, adults are by far the worst, especially if in positions of any power.'

Nan's thoughts flew to Miss Winter and the headmistress seemed to read her mind for she asked suddenly, 'I hope that you have had no more trouble with your drama mistress?'

'No,' lied Nan, glancing across at Wang Li, who was steadfastly avoiding the headmistress' gaze.

An Unpleasant Encounter

'Well, if you do, don't hesitate to tell either Miss Porter or myself,' went on Miss Montagu, 'And Wang Li, you say you do not understand bullies; believe me, my child, that is a thing to be thankful for. It means that you are as far removed from them as could be. And now, you really must be going to your common room. Your friends will be wondering where on earth you have got to.'

Nan and Wang Li went and were soon swallowed up to the pleasant noise and chatter of the common room. Elaine had put a record on the gramophone, and everyone was swizzling about to jolly Charleston music. Not wanting to break the mood or revisit their upset, Nan and Wang Li joined in the hilarity enthusiastically.

It was only later when they were alone in the dormitory together that Nan brought up something that was troubling her, 'You didn't tell Miss Montagu about Miss Winter.'

Wang Li looked at her slyly out of the corner of her eyes. 'Neither did you,' she observed coolly.

'I know,' Nan bit her lip, distressed, 'But I don't know what there is to say. I mean, at least with physical bullying it's tangible. You know where you are and it's easier to tell someone and be believed,' her voice trailed off.

'It's difficult,' agreed Wang Li, 'hard to put your finger on and Miss Winter is an adult and a teacher; if she denies it, we can't prove she's lying and she's always careful to be nice in front of the other mistresses.' A sudden exclamation burst from the girl, and she clapped a hand to her mouth, 'Oh, I've just remembered! Leonora said she had a plan to get rid of Miss Winter!'

'Really?' Nan felt a strange combination of curiosity, excitement and apprehension. 'Oh dear, I wonder what in the world she's planning?'

'I don't know; she wouldn't say. I just hope that it all goes to plan.'

The two girls looked at one another in consternation. Leonora meant well, but what if she just made things worse?

20

A Plan

The next day dawned crisp and fresh, a fine dusting of powdery snow dusting the lawns. A little, red-breasted robin hopped about, twittering joyfully at the dormitory window and Nan smiled, all the stress and anxiety of the previous day draining from her. She had had a bath before going to bed, wanting to wash away all trace of the horrid racist bullies of that afternoon, but she could not wash them out of her mind, and it had taken her a while to get to sleep with the taunts and insults playing over and over in her head. She had forced herself not to waste another thought on the hateful girls, however, and had instead thought with anticipation of Barbara's forthcoming midnight feast, soon falling into a deep and exhausted sleep.

Porcine Pranks at St. Anne's

Now she felt cleansed and refreshed. All throughout that day Nan and Millicent received congratulations from students and mistresses alike. Only Mamzelle, who did not see the point of Lacrosse, was stingy in her praise, saying, 'Oui, felicitations à Nan et à Millicent,' she said curtly, 'But now we must concentrate on our French grammar. No more word on the winning of this so-silly game or the poor girls' heads will be getting swollen.'

That weekend, all the first formers in Miss Porter's house walked into the village to buy a little something for Barbara for her birthday and some eatables to contribute to the feast. Leonora had still not been told by Miss Porter that she might leave the school grounds so she could not go.

'Do you think she's forgotten?' asked Beryl fretfully.

Leonora snorted derisively, 'I think she's forgotten on purpose.'

'Well,' said Barbara thoughtfully, 'it does seem a little harsh, but when you think of everything that she doesn't know about, I think you've got off pretty lightly.'

'Do you think she takes that into account- all the things she doesn't know about?' asked Leonora suspiciously.

'I should think she probably does,' laughed Barbara.

'That's unfair surely; she can't know that there are any other things.'

A Plan

'Well, I should think there are a lot more than she can possibly guess,' said Nan teasingly, 'What's all this I hear about a trick on Miss Winter?'

Leonora's eyes flitted over to where Beryl sat in the window seat counting her pocket money, 'Anyway,' she continued studiously avoiding Nan's question, 'it doesn't matter. Nan you can take my money into town and choose something nice for Barbara and buy a tin of condensed milk or two for the feast.' Leonora threw her purse at Nan who caught it deftly, 'And Barbara can stay here with me and keep me company.'

Barbara made a face at her friend before fetching out a jigsaw from the wet break cupboard at the back of the classroom, as Nan nodded eagerly and, linking arms with Poppy, disappeared downstairs. They could soon be seen from the window waving back at the two left in the first form classroom. Leonora did occasionally still visit the common room, but Miss Porter had taken to checking so it was safer to meet in the classroom.

Nan and Poppy relished these walks into the village and pitied Leonora for having to forego them. Both were glad to be muffled up today as the days were properly wintry now. The trees either side of the lane were now bare of leaves and stark against a sky of low clouds of a purple hue. A narrow bar of light seeped out on the horizon catching the few brittle leaves that still clung on. The rest of the leaves were heaped invitingly in the two ditches either side of the lane and Nan and Poppy crunched along in them. Beryl, Wang Li and Elaine followed suit, scooping up handfuls of leaves and hurling them at each other with whoops and squeals of delight. Daisy-May watched them longingly, evidently afraid such behaviour was beneath a head of form. A gaggle of stuffy fifth formers walked quickly past disdainfully, but Amrita and Isobel joined in heartily.

The first formers spent a happy afternoon in the village shops stopping for tea and cake at the China Pot Tea Shop and returning to school around four o'clock when it was already growing dark.

Elaine was swinging the wicker basket that contained all their purchases done up in brown paper and string, a skip in her step. Everyone's faces glowed rosy in the cold and there was a tantalising smell of chimney smoke in the air that promised a warm house to get back to. Nan felt a pleasant glow inside her. How lucky she was to go to St. Anne's and have such a lot of friends. And how lucky too to have tricks and midnight feasts to enjoy. She could hardly wait until Saturday.

On the first formers returning to school, Beryl was accosted just outside the gate to Miss Porter's house by Leonora who bid her to follow her to where they would not be disturbed. Intrigued, the others watched

A Plan

bemusedly as the two girls walked off in the direction of the stables.

'Well?' asked Leonora impatiently once they reached the cover of the fir trees.

'Well what?' Beryl looked utterly confused, 'you're the one that wanted to speak to me.'

'I know idiot! I meant did you find out what I asked you to?' queried Leonora, a desperate note in her voice.

Beryl's face cleared 'Oh that, I'd quite forgotten.' It had been some days now since Leonora had asked Beryl to find out by as round about way as possible what Miss Winter was afraid of.

'I bet you asked her straight out, didn't you?' scolded Leonora shaking her head despairingly.

'I did not!' countered Beryl, incensed to raising her voice.

'Shhh!' hissed Leonora in a loud stage whisper that quite put Beryl's exclamation in the shade.

'I did just as you said,' grumbled Beryl in quieter tones, 'I led up to it by saying that we had seen a horse and cart in the village and that I was scared of horses. I was quite silly about it, but eventually she confided in me.'

Beryl stopped suddenly, a smile starting out tentatively on her lips and then growing into a wide grin of suppressed mirth. Her eyes shone as she raised them to an infuriated Leonora.

'And?' prodded that girl, all her attention taut for the long-awaited information, 'What did she say? Come on, out with it, you chump! I'm cold, even if you're not.'

'You'll never guess!' wailed Beryl, seized by a fit of giggles that subsided under the other girl's stern gaze. She managed at last to gasp out, 'Pigs! She's scared of pigs!'

For a few moments both contemplated the munching Bobby at their feet the other side of the low wall. Leonora wore a dazed expression which transformed slowly into a tight-lipped smile and then an incredulous frown, 'Why is she scared of pigs?'

'Oh, Heaven knows!' shrieked Beryl before remembering that she could be counted alongside heaven as one of the lucky few, 'I remember now! She said that she had been bitten by one as a girl.'

'Bitten? By a pig?' echoed Leonora.

'Yes, and she said that she was scared of something else too- oh, what was it?'

'You really are quite hopeless, Beryl,' chided Leonora, 'This is the last time I get you involved in trick prep..'

'Was it ghosts?' Beryl was still trying to think.

'How should I know?'

'No, no, not ghosts…I know, it was thunderstorms!' cried Beryl triumphantly.

Leonora rolled her eyes, 'How can I create a thunderstorm? Are you even sure about the pig thing?'

A Plan

Beryl nodded emphatically, 'Oh, yes, I'd hardly forget that.'

'No, I suppose not. Well, thank you, we got there in the end. That is very interesting indeed Beryl. What a bit of luck for us that Miss Winter should prove to be scared of pigs!' And Leonora smiled a smile that is generally labelled a sinister smile.

21

A Pig in a Thunderstorm

Leonora wasted no time in putting her plan to the girls in Miss Porter's house. She chose a break time when they were all gathered around Bobby's pen outside the stables, petting her.

'I say, listen up, will you!' she demanded, raising her voice above the hubbub of chatter. 'I've got the most wonderful plan to get rid of Miss Winter,' she added lowering her voice conspiratorially.

Everyone stared at her. Daisy-May looked aghast, Beryl hysterical, Nan nervous, Poppy and Barbara interested and Wang Li sceptical.

'Beryl's found out that she is scared of pigs,' continued Leonora, eying Poppy with a measure of apprehension, 'So, I am going to need your permission

Poppy to borrow Bobby- just for a few minutes.' Leonora turned beseeching eyes upon the girl, but Poppy refused to be taken in. 'All she'd have to do would be to be seen, that's all,' continued Leonora earnestly.

'Where?' Poppy put her finger on the nub of the matter in her downright way.

'In Miss Winter's bedroom,' answered Leonora promptly to gasps of dismay from her classmates.

'Goodness,' marvelled Barbara in grudging admiration, 'Who would dare?'

'Leonora,' cried Daisy-May weakly in a voice that was little more than a croak, 'you can't- you simply can't break into a mistress' bedroom and put a pig in there!'

'I can,' Leonora assured her steadfastly, 'And what's more I intend to. You needn't be held responsible for me if things go wrong. Get yourself off to the san. with a sore throat and you won't even have to be in the dorm tonight. We sleep in separate dorms anyhow, so I don't see the problem.'

Really thought Daisy-May, no one could be responsible for Leonora-she just went her own way and damned the consequences.

Wang Li was arching her dark eyebrows at the girl, the salient points of this little speech not lost on her, 'Tonight?' she queried astutely.

Leonora reddened, 'Yes, well, I don't see why we should waste any more time about it.'

Porcine Pranks at St. Anne's

Elaine clapped her hands joyously 'Oh, what a good lark it will be! I wish I could go with you!'

Daisy-May groaned inwardly; what a job she had as head of the first form! 'We could just tell Miss Porter...' she suggested in a small voice. She was ignored, Leonora miming a large yawn and the word, 'boring'.

Wang Li was frowning thoughtfully and now she said, 'Leonora surely you are not the best person to carry out this plan. Would Bobby follow your lead? We have to be certain that she will. No, I think either Nan or Poppy or both should go.'

Leonora looked more than a little put out by this change of plan for she had been looking forward to her midnight adventure, but she saw that Wang Li's reasoning was sound; she could not be sure that Bobby would do as she said.

Nan was looking at Poppy to see what she thought of this idea. To her surprise the girl was trying hard to suppress a laugh, seeming utterly taken with this plan. Nan herself was torn between apprehension and excitement. There were so many things that could go wrong, but in the end her desire to get one over on Miss Winter triumphed and she let her face break into a broad grim of acquiescence. 'What about yourself Wang Li?' she asked thinking how the Chinese girl had suffered at Miss Winter's hands.

'Oh no,' said Wang Li quickly, 'I think two people are

quite enough. You can tell me all about it tomorrow.'

'That's settled then,' said Poppy warmly, 'Nan and I will do it!'

The first formers generally went up to bed at half past eight to get in half an hour's reading time before Matron came in at nine o'clock for lights out.

Once Matron had gone on her way, they allowed her half an hour to get settled back in her own room. Then they put their plan into action.

Earlier in the evening, Leonora had revealed to them her rope of tied together old sheets which she had made at the beginning of term and which she had been using to sneak out of her own common room without alerting Matron or Miss Sparks. She had smuggled it out of Miss Sparks' house coiled in the bottom of her needlework basket and Nan had then taken charge of it, placing it under her clothes in the chest at the bottom of her bed from whence she and Poppy now took it.

'I say,' whispered Poppy, 'it's heavier than you'd think, isn't it?'

'Shh!' hissed Nan desperately; she couldn't believe what they were about to do.

Barbara flitted from her bed, a dark shadow, and helped the other two to open the window, and, having checked the coast was clear, lower the makeshift rope out into the night. Nan hooked the thoughtfully looped end around the foot of her bed which was nearest the window. It took the strength of all three girls to lift it a couple of inches.

'Well, that should hold your weight all right,' panted Barbara, sitting down on her bed after the effort, 'Who'll go first?'

'I will,' volunteered Nan, who, now that she was actually doing it was brimming with an excitable energy at their late-night adventure. 'And Barbara, you had jolly well better remember about us when we want to get back in!'

'I will, don't you worry,' Barbara reassured her, 'I've got a book to read, but I'll keep checking the window. For Heaven's sake don't throw any gravel up. Matron may sleep like a log, but Miss Porter's ears are as sharp as anything.'

With nothing else to say, Nan went over to the window. The night air was chilly, and a little shiver passed over her. There was a moon, but it was not full. Everything looked sinister in the dark, shadows looming out, hiding the scene she knew so well in daylight and twisting it into unfamiliar shapes.

Steadying herself, Nan put out a hand and gripped the sheet rope. It was long way down, but Nan had never been scared of heights. Turning, she sat down on the windowsill before lowering herself out over the ground and abseiling down. It felt very daring, and Nan felt a little thrill as her feet unexpectedly touched the ground.

Poppy immediately followed, but instead of abseiling, she clung to the rope with arms and legs. She didn't so much swarm down as slither, landing gracelessly in a dizzy heap at Nan's feet. Laughing silently at her friend's peculiar style, Nan helped her to her feet and dusted her down. The sheets were already disappearing rapidly back up through the window as Barbara hauled them in for it wouldn't do to leave them out for everyone to see.

Poppy had a torch in her pocket, but they shouldn't need one for the lights from the school sent a warm orange glow seeping out to meet them, lighting their path quite sufficiently.

As they reached the stables and saw Bobby tucking into a late supper, the enormity of their imminent crime struck Nan and she half thought of turning back but glancing at Poppy's grim set face and glinting eyes, she realised that her friend was game and would not be dissuaded.

She didn't so much swam down as slither.

A Pig in a Thunderstorm

Remembering every unkind word, every angry threat, every pointed disregard of Miss Winter's, Nan felt the anger seethe up in her, fuelling her determination to do something in retaliation.

Bobby appeared reluctant to leave her bran mash and oats, but on realising that it was her mistress come to see her so unexpectedly, she readily acquiesced to a little mid-supper walk, trotting eagerly between the two girls.

Avoiding the main entrance, the trio advanced hearts in mouths to the back door. Seized by a sudden terrible thought, Nan wondered if it may be locked already, but no, it swung invitingly open at Poppy's touch.

Entering quickly to avoid being spotted from the outside, the friends now faced the prospect of being spotted on the inside. They made hurriedly for the back stairs, trying to keep their footsteps as soundless as possible on the tiled floor. Bobby, however, had other ideas, and clattered off in the direction of the kitchens, her trotters sounding agonisingly loud on the ceramic.

Poppy flew noiselessly after her pet and with a little persuasive patting and prodding managed to get her to mount the stairs. This was hard going with trotters, but Bobby made it and the strange little group took a breather on the landing. Petrified of meeting a housemaid or, even worse, a mistress, they listened intently before progressing down the corridor that led to the large art and sewing room, and off which were mistresses' studies and bedrooms for those who slept in School House.

Bobby, for some unknown reason, threatened suddenly to break into a wild canter the length of the corridor, but Poppy held on tight to her wriggling form. Although still relatively small in size, Bobby was too heavy for Poppy to lift comfortably for any length of time.

Aware of their exposed position, Nan crept on down the long, narrow corridor. Poppy followed suit with Bobby hugged to her chest. That corridor seemed to the two girls to stretch on for ever. They inched along it counting off the studies on one side, the bedrooms on the other. Half-way down was an alcove with a useful curtain across it and into this welcome cover the trio rushed.

And not a moment too soon for no sooner had Bobby's curly tail disappeared behind the green velvet, than a door flew open to their left and Mamzelle Meuhourat lumbered out yawning widely.

'Oh la la! Ma tête!' she cried theatrically, 'she will take no more work tonight. I am off to bed. Bonne nuit, mademoiselle Porter.'

Poppy risked a peep out.

'Good night Mamzelle,' came Miss Porter's voice from inside the little study where she was finishing off a stack of marking.

Nan and Poppy exchanged horrified glances inside the murky interior of the alcove and by silent agreement waited some three minutes though to Nan it felt like an eternity.

Poppy risked a peep out, and no one being in sight, ushered Nan and Bobby on to the other end of the corridor where Miss Winter had her sleeping quarters.

'You're sure it's this door?' mouthed Nan.

'Positive,' breathed Poppy back.

Nan laid a tentative hand on the handle. To her surprise it gave. Alarmed Nan wondered if the drama mistress could be inside, but no sound came from within. Pushing the door open silently, Nan found that the room was empty. It was not a large room, but its emptiness made it seem larger than it was. A narrow bed was pushed up against the wall to the left-hand side. In the middle wall was a small square window and to the right a walk-in cupboard and a chest of drawers. On top of the drawers was a revoltingly lumpy handbag that accompanied the mistress everywhere. Its presence in the room explained to Nan the reason for the door being unlocked. Miss Winter had already been in and put down her handbag, but she must have nipped out again for something that she had forgotten. Why, she might return at any second!

Having realised all this in a matter of seconds, Nan beckoned Poppy and Bobby in frantically before shutting the door behind them. She already fancied she heard footsteps in the passage without. Now they were trapped inside with nowhere to hide.

Not quite nowhere. Alarmed, Nan swept the room with a searching glance and spotted the large cupboard door. Poppy, as panicked as she was, had the same thought, and opened it quickly to reveal a wardrobe of square floorspace.

Both girls dived inside, shutting the door firmly behind them and made themselves as comfortable as possible on the floor, the perfume drenched dresses tickling their faces and their hearts beating like wild beasts inside their ribcages. Bobby was left on the other side of the door, wondering fearfully what had become of her mistress.

Nan strained her ears to hear above her pounding heart. For a little while all that could be heard was Bobby emitting small grunts and squeals as she snuffled about the unfamiliar space in desperate search of her mistress. Then the door to the little bedroom opened with a click and a creak, and Miss Winter could be heard taking a couple of steps inside. Then came a second of dead silence shattered by a short sharp scream of terror and the heavy banging of the door as the terrified drama mistress fled in panic.

Porcine Pranks at St. Anne's

As soon as they heard her take this abrupt leave, Nan and Poppy burst from the heady perfumed space of the wardrobe before scurrying from the room, a delighted Bobby at their heels.

Out in the corridor the trio made straight for the alcove, glad that Miss Winter had disappeared inside one of the other rooms but conscious that they had only seconds before she reappeared with reinforcements.

They made it behind the curtain just in time, for, moments later, the door to Mamzelle Meuhourat's and Miss Porter's study was flung open, and Miss Winter came stumbling blindly out. Her eyes were staring, her hair dishevelled, and she was repeating her pleas for assistance over and over in desperate tones.

Miss Porter laid down her pen, glanced at the clock on the wall and followed the drama mistress at a leisurely pace that Miss Winter clearly found infuriating. 'Hurry! Oh, hurry! It has probably eaten the bedclothes by now!' sobbed the mistress, clutching at her hair as though she would tear it out.

'Miss Winter, it is hardly likely that a pig can have found its way into your room,' said Miss Porter in what she imagined to be soothing tones.

'I tell you it-' Miss Winter stopped short as she reached the open door and took in the utterly pigless state of the interior. 'It was here,' she said defiantly forestalling her colleague's assurances to the contrary.

'How big was this pig?' asked Miss Porter as one who plays along with the fantasy of the insane.

'It was massive, and strong,' avowed a hysterical Miss Winter, 'This big!' she added, flinging out her arms to indicate a dimension only a dozen inches short of the room itself.

Miss Porter, thinking of the only pig she knew of on the premises, felt her conscience recede. Bobby was not half as large as that. Besides it was absurd. To smuggle a pig up a flight of stairs, past her own study door and into a mistress' bedroom! She did not credit any in her form with such foolhardiness. She would check that Bobby was safe and sound in the stables on her way back home, and if so, that would satisfy her.

Miss Winter, meanwhile, was engaged in having mild hysterics. They were mild only because she would have preferred a more attentive audience.

'And how on Earth is an animal that size to pass down this corridor without my hearing it?' demanded Miss Porter, vexed that her colleague could credit her with so deficient a sense of hearing.

Miss Winter stopped, gradually, to have hysterics, and turned the question over in her mind for a satisfactory answer. 'The window!' she exclaimed, jumping up and trying it, 'It's unlocked!' she observed as if that answered everything.

The first form mistress raised an eyebrow or two

and then poured an icy bucket of scorn on this idea, 'Pigs do not have wings!'

Miss Winter's face fell then she frowned and opened her mouth as though to argue the point. Miss Porter, however, had had enough, and after a few well-chosen words on the effect of overwork on a tired brain producing hallucinations -Leonora would have been proud of her- she left the room and strode briskly back to her study to collect her things. At the alcove she stopped and, on an impulse, twitched back the curtains.

It was empty.

Nan, Poppy and Bobby were long gone.

As soon as Nan had seen the two mistresses enter the bedroom, the trio had fled noiselessly down the corridor, down the backstairs and out into the night, the still air like ice against their faces. From the distant hills rolled a huge bellow of thunder followed by a flash of lightning that lit the scene, making dramatic shadows. Afraid of being caught out in the rain that threatened from the storm laden clouds, the two friends hurried as fast as they could, their feet pounding into the earth with each energetic leap.

The rope of knotted sheets swung out of the first-floor window before they'd even quite made it back from depositing Bobby at the stables. Barbara must have been watching at the window.

When they climbed up and collapsed into the room with the exhilaration of their completed mission, Barbara was curled up in bed. The bedclothes over her head, she held a torch in one hand and *A Damsel in Distress* by P. G. Wodehouse in the other.

'Did you, do it?' she asked, studying their shining faces.

'Yes,' breathed Nan hardly believing herself.

When she awoke next morning after a deep sleep, she supposed the events of the past night to have been merely a most peculiar dream. It was only when she looked across at Poppy and saw the exact same expression on her face that she realised it was true.

22

Mamzelle's Niece

When the first formers trouped up to their classroom the following day for their first lesson of the week, Miss Porter did not appear for form until five minutes before Mamzelle Meuhourat was due to take them for French. When she did appear, she seemed distracted, 'I'm sorry I'm late girls, but I have been with Miss Montagu. It appears that Miss Winter will not be taking you for drama again this term.'

There was a collected gasp at this happy news and Nan and Poppy exchanged mirthful glances.

'Why, whatever's happened?' asked Millicent without thinking to raise her hand, 'Is she ill?'

'No,' answered the first form mistress, too distrait to censure her and instead revealing perhaps a little more than she ought, 'Miss Winter left a note saying that she had got up early to get a taxi to the train station where she was taking a train away from us- for good.'

'She's left!' cried Beryl, 'Just like that!'

'How very strange,' murmured Barbara.

'Yes, I wonder *why* she's left,' pondered Leonora, frowning.

Miss Porter shot her a suspicious glance, 'Yes, indeed,' she said, 'I don't suppose we shall ever know.'

'Just one of Life's little mysteries,' mused Barbara wickedly.

'Not unless she'd like to tell us,' put in Leonora.

'Well, she'll be sorely missed,' sniggered Beryl, making Elaine snort with explosive laughter.

Miss Porter quelled her with a look, 'I had no idea you found your drama mistress so diverting. I think that will do, don't you? You can take out your French books for Mamzelle will be along in a moment.'

Everyone sat up to attention in expectation of Mamzelle Meuhourat and her reaction to this latest piece of news. The French mistress did not disappoint. She tottered into the room perched on her high heels, felt her way to the desk and collapsed onto her chair dramatically, 'Ah, mes enfants! You will not guess what has occurred!'

'Yes; Miss Winter's left,' said Millicent glibly, causing Mamzelle Meuhourat to visibly deflate.

'Ah, mademoiselle Porter, she has already told you, n'est-ce pas?' she said reproachfully.

'She didn't tell us why Miss Winter left,' prompted Wang Li innocently.

It was all that Mamzelle needed. 'Then you know nothing!' she cried triumphantly before launching into a confused account, 'Mademoiselle Winter, last night, she is in such a state! She suffers, it seems, from the halloocinasions. The poor woman, she was convinced- but convinced- that there was a pig in her bedroom. I cub you not-'

'Kid, Mamzelle,' piped Barbara.

'Cub or kid- c'est égal,' opined the French mistress shortly, eager to continue her interrupted narrative, 'A pig, that is what she swore she saw in her chambre de lit, and not just a mignonne such as was once in this classroom. Non- but a great big pig. Un sanglier such as we have in France!'

'A wild boar,' translated Wang Li for the benefit of the others.

'Oui, c'est ça,' agreed Mamzelle, smiling on her favourite, 'Well, of such an animal there was no trace, but mademoiselle Winter, she remains convinced. She will not sleep in her bed. She demands instead a different room. She complains bitterly of the noise of the thunder. And then, this morning, the chambermaid she finds a note upon her pillow to say that she is gone! Oh la la!'

Mamzelle's Niece

'Oh Mamzelle!' cried Beryl sympathetically, 'it must have been a great shock to you!'

'Oui, bien sûr,' admitted Mamzelle soberly, 'C'était tellement étonnant. My poor nerves! With my poor niece ill, they will not take much more strain.'

Everyone exchanged alarmed looks at this. Of course, Matron had told them at the beginning of term that Mamzelle's niece had been supposed to be in the first with them but had been taken ill. And yet not one of them had spared a thought for either Mamzelle or her niece. The first formers suddenly felt extremely uncomfortable. Why, they had done everything in their power calculated to upset Mamzelle's nerves with all their horrid unfeeling tricks! What must the poor French mistress have been feeling?

'Oh, poor Mamzelle!' sobbed Beryl, her kind heart easily touched, 'We are so very sorry we ever played those tricks on you.'

Mamzelle Meuhourat looked around her at the taut guilty faces and gave a broad reassuring smile, 'Do not make yourselves inquiet, mes enfants,' she said, 'Your tricks- they make me anxious for a moment perhaps, but they make me to laugh. En fait, I look back on them fondly as you say. And Élise, my niece, she is also very taken with them. I write and tell her all my news, and when you have played me a trick the news it is so much more interesting.'

Porcine Pranks at St. Anne's

'Juicy,' supplied Leonora, grinning.

Mamzelle frowned not quite understanding this.

'How is your niece, Mamzelle,' asked Nan, relieved to hear that Élise got so much pleasure from Mamzelle's tales of St. Anne's.

'My niece,' sighed Mamzelle, 'Alas, she has been very poorly, hein. She has suffered from the tuberculosis and her lungs they will perhaps never be what they once were. But she is through the worst of it, and she makes progress, the little one. My brother proposes to take her into the mountains to recuperate. There she will have the fresh air and the warm healing spring waters.'

Everyone looked very subdued. They had not thought Élise's illness so bad. Leonora was looking unusually concerned.

'When will Élise be able to come to St. Anne's?' asked Wang Li tentatively.

'Not for a year, I fear,' said Mamzelle gravely, 'the poor child- she has been very ill, and she has lost a lot of her strength.' An idea struck the French mistress and she brightened, 'But you may write to Élise. It will help your French, and Élise- once she feels able- can reply in English for she must practice her English.'

'Oh, yes Mamzelle, of course we will write!' cried Nan eagerly, and Wang Li and Barbara nodded too. Even Poppy, for whom French was a difficult subject, agreed to write, 'She'll laugh if I mess it up!' she chuckled good-naturedly.

Some of the others were less keen but felt so guilty at their prior inattentiveness that they determined to write at least once if only to introduce themselves to their soon-to-be classmate. Mamzelle was so overjoyed at their interest in her niece that she readily forgave them for having wasted half the lesson chatting.

That week was taken up with preparations for Barbara's birthday feast which was to be on the Saturday. It was agreed that it would be held in the common room as any crumbs were more easily explained away there. The question arose as to what they would have to drink, and Beryl answered it by going down to the kitchens to ask Cook.

'I say, Cookie, dear,' she began, making her eyes wide and pleading.

'Yes, Miss Beryl?' grumbled Cook expectantly.

'Do you think you could possibly let me have two big jugs of lemonade on Saturday? You can just leave them on the kitchen table when you go home. Please?'

'My Goodness, Miss Beryl! You'll never drink all that lot on your own!' exclaimed Cook, studying the small girl appraisingly, 'And why Saturday night?' she added archly.

'Oh, I will drink it Cookie!' cried Beryl, then added

in sly inconsequence, 'I feel I'll get a terrible thirst on Saturday night.'

'Oh, do you, you young rascal? I should report this. Don't think I don't know what you and your friends are up to,' she scolded, but there was a roguish twinkle in her eye.

'Well of course you know Cookie,' flattered Beryl at once, 'You're clever, but if I don't tell you, you can say you didn't know, can't you?'

'Now, now,' said Cook, putting down a rolling pin and wiping floury hands on her apron, 'did I say I wouldn't do as you asked, Miss Beryl? If you clear out of my kitchen now and let me get dinner ready, I'll let you have three jugs of lemonade!'

'Thanks awfully Cookie; you're the best!' cried a joyful Beryl as she sped from the kitchens.

Another thing to happen that week was the away Lacrosse match against Miss Martineau's School for Young Ladies. Amrita went after all; she persuaded Miss Montagu that she had to take her own risks, to which the headmistress had sighed and said, 'You're right of course. I forget that I cannot keep you all safe. One day- very soon in your case, Amrita- you will go out into the world, and you must be prepared for the harsh reality of this life. We will all meet many people over the course of our lifetimes who we do not agree with, and we must learn to deal with it. Go then, if you must, but be careful.'

Nan felt glad that she was not obliged to play and even gladder when Millicent returned to fill in the rest of her form on the events of that horrendous match. The girl was clutching a ferocious nosebleed and from the mood of the returning team one would have felt that they had lost, but they had in fact won three goals to nil. A win that secured the title for St. Anne's.

'Well done old thing!' cheered Leonora, clapping her on the back. Millicent winced and gratefully took the clean handkerchief that Nan was mutely holding out to her.

'How was it?' asked Nan tentatively, though she could guess the answer well enough.

'It was a bloodbath!' answered Millicent thickly, 'we've accrued more injuries in that one match than all season. They were out to get us this time. It's a jolly good thing you let well alone, or I honestly believe they would have done their utmost to murder you! Miss Knight is absolutely furious. She wanted to stop the match, but we decided we had to play on and make sure we beat them.'

Nan looked across to the charabancs and saw Miss Knight helping the rest of the battered team down. She had never seen the young mistress so angry. She was always so patient and bubbling over with a happy

Porcine Pranks at St. Anne's

energy and enthusiasm. The look on her face now was murderous, her eyes looked daggers and her mouth was set in a grim line.

'Well, you certainly beat them,' stated Barbara, 'Three nil; that's the best result of the season.'

'It was hard won,' said Millicent from behind her blood-soaked hanky, 'Their goalie gave me this after I scored the winning goal, and another of the goal scorers, Grace, got a black eye for her troubles. Someone managed to catch Heather across the shins with their Lacrosse stick and she's still hobbling.'

'What about Amrita?' asked Nan anxiously, 'I can't see her; is she all right?'

'Oh, Amrita's fine,' Millicent assured her, 'Just mad with rage. She stuck close to Miss Knight the whole time, and no one dared go for her there. Even if they did, I believe she was so angry she'd have given as good as she got, but luckily it didn't turn into a free-for-all. Miss Knight went for their games mistress like anything though- you should have seen her- she was marvellous. She's going to get Miss Montagu to write to the Heads of St. Catherine's and Miss Lindsey's and get them to boycott Miss Martineau's too.'

'What a school!' phewed Barbara, 'I'm glad I don't go there. It only opened very recently and its already getting a reputation. Apparently, girls don't even have to do proper lessons, but can just turn up if they want.

Talk about undisciplined! And this violence is the result! I'm mightily glad you won't have to play against them anymore, the devils!'

'Yes, well, I'd better be going off to Matron. See you,' observed Millicent and veered off, still trying to stem the steady flow from her nose.

23

A Midnight Feast

The rest of the week passed with the first formers growing ever more restless in anticipation of the feast. At long last Saturday was upon them, and the morning was spent clustered around Barbara as she opened her presents. They were only small things as pocket money would allow, but much appreciated, nevertheless. They consisted of a bag of sweets from Beryl, a bar of chocolate from Daisy-May, *The Secret of Chimneys* by Agatha Christie from Wang Li and a silk square for cleaning glasses from Nan with the beautifully embroidered initials B. W. in the corner. Poppy contributed a tin of hair pins. From Leonora the birthday girl received two pairs of thick woollen socks and from Elaine a bar of lavender scented soap.

A Midnight Feast

The day was spent alternatively walking through the frosty stubbled fields and sitting by the warm flickering flames of the common room fire, swathed in blankets, each absorbed in her own page-turner.

Nan thought it a jolly good thing that Barbara's birthday did not fall on a weekday for she simply wouldn't have been able to concentrate during lessons.

The day seemed to stretch on and on, but at last a suitably advanced hour arrived at which to retire to bed. Matron was most surprised and suspicious to see the first formers trooping off to their dormitory at eight o'clock. Beryl gave her a large, prolonged yawn which only served to increase her suspicion.

Barbara carefully set her alarum clock for ten minutes to midnight, burrowing it safely under her two large pillows and bolster to muffle the ringing. No one felt at all tired and Elaine vowed she would not go to sleep. There was much excited giggling and whispering, but eventually everyone, even Elaine, fell into deep contented sleeps and only woke on Barbara's urgently shaking them. 'Psst! Midnight feast!' was hissed into each girl's ear and repeated in ecstatic anticipation.

Nan sat up at once, shocked to have fallen asleep after all and full of excitement for her first midnight feast. At her bedside, Barbara's tall figure in its ghostly nightdress put a warning finger to its lips. Slipping bare feet into eagerly waiting slippers, Nan swung herself

Porcine Pranks at St. Anne's

into her cosy dressing gown which had lain expectantly across her bed. She then padded about the darkened room, helping Barbara to wake the others and at last they were all ready.

In a state of suppressed excitement, the little group made their way cautiously out onto the landing and across to the door of the common room. Nan and Barbara crept to the airing cupboard door at the end of the landing, and opening it, passed the hidden goodies within to the others as they filed past.

Eventually everyone was settled in the common room, laying out the food on the three small tables about the room. It was as Barbara softly shut the door, that a small persistent knocking came from the direction of one of the curtained windows. Poppy, who was nearest, disappeared behind the heavy curtains, and pushing up the lower sash of the window, came face to face with Leonora who was balancing at the top of a tall ladder purloined from the gardener.

'I hope you don't mind but I brought Millicent along with me,' said Leonora in sepulchral tones, and looking down, Poppy saw that Millicent was indeed waiting her turn at the bottom of the ladder, a brown paper package under one arm.

Stepping aside, Poppy allowed both girls to climb inside before noiselessly closing the window after them. Daisy-May looked on in consternation but said nothing.

Millicent offered her paper parcel to Barbara with a word of apology for her unexpected arrival.

'It's no matter,' Barbara reassured her in a low voice, 'There's more than enough food to go around. Hello!' she exclaimed as she tore off the brown paper wrapping to reveal a copy of *Piccadilly Jim* by P. G. Wodehouse. 'I say, thanks awfully! However did you know I hadn't this one?'

'I quizzed Leonora,' replied Millicent getting out of her heavy felt coat and laying it across a chair. Underneath their winter coats, she and Leonora both wore pyjamas and dressing gowns.

'I'm starving!' groaned Beryl, and then clapped a hand over her mouth as she remembered not to make a sound.

'You're right, we'd best get a move on, it's a quarter past twelve already,' said Leonora beginning to hand round napkins. 'Beryl, where's that lemonade you promised?'

'Oh Goodness, yes!' exclaimed Beryl, 'I went and fetched it from the kitchens with Elaine after tea, oh, where did we put it? Can you remember, Elaine?'

'Gosh, no, whatever did we do with it?' cried a fretful Elaine.

Barbara rolled her eyes, 'You two really are the absolute limit!'

'I remember seeing you putting something into that cupboard,' remarked Nan helpfully, pointing to a large

Porcine Pranks at St. Anne's

cupboard in the corner where spare notebooks and ink was stored. Leonora opened it and there were the three jugs of lemonade.

'Well, fancy! They *are* here!' observed Leonora in awed tones, and promptly passed them to Poppy who diligently filled everybody's bedside mug.

Soon the feast was in full swing. There were all sorts of delicious things: tinned peaches, tinned sardines, shortbread biscuits, warm squidgy gingerbread, oranges, condensed milk, and the centrepiece, Barbara's birthday cake, a chocolate affair with buttercream bursting out of its middle. The first formers had all eaten sparingly at tea so as to have room for their feast, but even so they would never be able to manage it all, though Beryl gave it her best shot.

'Phew,' said Wang Li, sitting back on her heels, and surveying the remains of the scrumptious feast, 'I couldn't eat another thing!'

'Me neither,' agreed Nan, lolling back in her chair.

Barbara glanced at her watch, 'Its five minutes to one,' she announced, 'Come on, lets shift this stuff back to the airing cupboard,' she added, obviously anxious to get rid of all the evidence of the successful feast as soon as possible.

'Have mercy,' moaned Beryl from her position stretched out on the carpeted floor, 'I couldn't possibly move for at least ten minutes!'

'I'll help you, Barbara!' cried Elaine eagerly, getting up and, in her haste, stepping on a plate containing the sticky crumbs that were all that was left of the gingerbread. She careered along before ploughing poor Poppy in the midriff, the China plate shattering. Poppy let out an aggrieved woof and, overbalancing, knocked into a heavy chair which fell over with a crash that sounded ear-splitting in the silence.

The girls stared at each other, horror-stricken. 'Oh! I'm so sorry!' breathed Elaine, looking ready to burst into tears.

'Well, that's torn it,' muttered Barbara decisively, 'Leonora, Millicent, you had better be off; if Miss Porter catches you both here, she'll have a fit.'

'I doubt it,' Leonora began to argue humorously, her momentary alarm gone, then she saw the serious look in her friend's eye and decided to humour her. 'All right, come along, Millicent, let's go.'

'Thank you,' whispered Millicent warmly as she stepped towards the window, 'It was a marvellous feast. Good luck!'

Barbara shut the window and drew the curtains behind them, listening intently all the while. No approaching footsteps could be heard, however. It would appear that the chair had not made such a very loud noise as they had first feared.

Everyone got up and helped drag a protesting Beryl

'Have mercy,' moaned Beryl from her position stretched out on the carpeted floor.

to her feet before bundling everything into the two big baskets from whence it had come. Any crumbs were hastily swept under the furniture, as Barbara cast about the room to check all was as it should be.

'Psst, Barbara, what should I do with these?' asked Wang Li, holding up Leonora and Millicent's coats one on each arm, which they had left in their haste.

'Blow!' cursed Barbara in heartfelt tones, 'Thanks Wang Li, if it wasn't for your sharp eyes Matron or Miss Porter would certainly have found them.' Leonora's coat was a distinctive orange colour, not unlike her hair. 'I'll bung them in the bottom of the airing cupboard, no one ever goes in there. There's only spare bedding in there and the housemaids change that as infrequently as they can get away with. If they get dusty it's their own faults for being ass enough to leave them.'

In just under five minutes, Nan was flicking off the electric light switch and closing the common room door before tiptoeing after the others along the darkened landing. Moving through the equally dark dormitory, Nan heard the muffled giggles of Beryl.

'Oh, Goodness, Barbara, I've just put my hand in my dressing gown pocket and there's a cream bun in there!'

'Well wherever from?' hissed Barbara's sharp voice, 'We haven't had any cream buns!'

'So we haven't!' chuckled Beryl, 'Well, I wonder how it got there, whatever ought I to do with it?'

'Get rid of it quick!'

'How?'

'Eat it,' advised Wang Li logically.

'Oh, but I couldn't!' cried Beryl in distressed tones.

'Put it under your pillow,' suggested Daisy-May who had been very quiet all night. Nan had thought her very weary and had seen her lips move as though in prayer at several junctures. The head girl had obviously given up trying to restrain her irrepressible form and was instead seeking divine influence to cope with the strain.

'Oh, no don't Beryl!' she contradicted herself now, 'It'll leave such a sticky mess!'

'Well, what should I do?' wailed Beryl.

'Put it with the other food in the cupboard and for Heaven's sake be careful about it!' snapped Barbara.

Beryl looked petrified, but slunk out obediently, and was soon back again looking pleased with herself.

At last, all the first formers were safely tucked up in bed and it wasn't long before most of them were asleep.

Barbara and Daisy-May stayed awake a little longer, fearful lest their midnight adventure had been overheard. But no rushing footsteps sounded, and they were able to conclude that their first midnight feast had passed off successfully. Smiling thankfully at such a wonderful birthday feast, Barbara closed her eyes and was soon dreaming.

24

Snowballs and Philosophy

Nan awoke the next day to the shrill ringing of the dressing-bell. Sitting up slowly, she rubbed her eyes. The others were all looking equally sluggish after their night-time escapade. Beryl had clasped her pillow over her head to deaden the noise, 'I thought it was the weekend!' she complained reproachfully.

'It is, it's Sunday,' said Wang Li who was already pulling on a woollen frock over thick woollen stockings, 'Church.'

'Church! Dear God, not that!' cried Beryl tragically and then leapt out of bed as Matron came bustling in, 'Why couldn't you have had your birthday on a Friday?' she hissed at Barbara before dutifully splashing cold water on her face and hands.

Porcine Pranks at St. Anne's

'Remind me next year,' answered Barbara, smiling grimly.

Despite Matron's best efforts, the first formers were late downstairs, missing breakfast, a state of affairs for which many were grateful. They only caught up with the rest of the school at the church doors where Miss Porter was waiting to usher them inside with a few sharp words.

Marching hurriedly between the pews, Nan caught sight of Millicent with a somewhat green Leonora who was doubled up after overeating the previous night.

The vicar popped up above the pulpit and proceeded on a long, dreary sermon about the good of mankind and resisting the propensity to selfish and material thoughts during the yuletide season. A sermon which had half the girls falling asleep, Beryl among them, and the other half in suppressed titters of laughter. Only the staid sixth formers gave the poor vicar their full and undivided attention. The vicar was quite at a loss to understand how his sermon could be so funny and, pushing his pince-nez further up the long bridge of his nose, endeavoured to continue, saying sternly, 'I trust that each of you whilst enjoying the fextravagant elicities-' Poppy gave a snort of laughter at this, earning herself a reproachful glare from the second form mistress, Miss Rowan. 'Ahm, excuse me,' went on the vicar, '-the, the *celebrations*- that you will spare a thought for those less fortunate than yourselves,' he finished in a hurry.

Wang Li thought of her country in the midst of its turbulent and disruptive civil war and hoped that the family she had left behind her might be spared too challenging a time.

Barbara's thoughts went to Élise Meuhourat, and she said a silent prayer for her swift recovery. When she opened her eyes, the sermon was just reaching a straggling conclusion.

The vicar proposed a hymn before stepping thankfully down from the pulpit, his robes rustling in the brief silence afforded before Mrs Deary scuttled to her place at the organ and began booming out the opening chords to Hark the Herald Angels Sing. Everyone rose to their feet and Nan and Poppy sung at the top of their lungs for Nan loved singing and Poppy certainly had a bracing voice. This particular hymn, however, was almost too much for Beryl and Leonora who were beginning to attract attention. Beryl got the giggles and emitted a curious shriek that made the vicar direct a very strange look at her which only made her more hysterical. Leonora on the other hand, was really looking very ill, and only the thought of Matron with her feared bottle of medicine got the girl through that service. It was not until the following morning that she felt truly better.

Porcine Pranks at St. Anne's

There were now just one and a half weeks until the Christmas holidays, and all of a sudden St. Anne's was becoming festive. In the spacious hallway, a local pine tree had been dragged in by a small army of groundsmen who did a marvellous job of manoeuvring it into an upright position. Housemaids, mistresses and sixth formers then all took a hand in decorating it, and the result was really excellent.

'Oh, isn't it beautiful!' gasped Beryl, gazing at its shimmering lights with starry eyes.

'Yes, the sixth have done a grand job,' agreed Barbara, coming down the stairs to stand admiringly next to it. It stood in state, adorned with golden stars, huge taffeta bows, tactfully spaced candles and oranges and nuts that became fewer as the week wore on.

'I preferred it bare,' said Poppy rather wistfully.

'Bare! Oh, no, Poppy!' shrilled Beryl in protest.

'I agree it does look splendid *au natural*,' said Barbara the peacemaker, 'But you must admit it has been done very tastefully.'

'Yes,' Poppy agreed grudgingly, 'There's nothing worse than an over-ornamented tree.'

'Do you suppose that fruit's imitation?' Leonora wanted to know.

'Wax, d'you mean?' said Barbara, 'I don't know. Smell it.'

Nan was soon in a position to ascertain that the

fruit was indeed real for she actually caught Miss Sparks helping herself to an orange and stared at her incredulously until, having peeled it she held out a segment to the astonished girl, 'For your silence,' she said mischievously, adding a second and then a third segment for good measure. Nan accepted them, dazed and then, noting Miss Sparks' absence, hastily left the scene of the crime before anyone happened upon her eating the tree's decoration.

The heady smell of pine permeated the whole school mingling with the rich, spicey aroma of batches and batches of mince pies and cinnamon biscuits which seemed always to be being baked.

The first formers were engaged in producing paper chains and other decorations during the lesson they would normally have had drama. There had been talk of them joining with the St. Becket's boys for drama, but in the end, drama had been dropped entirely in favour of crafts since Miss Whyte was free and eager for some willing helpers.

Music lessons were now spent rehearsing carols and assemblies became extra practice sessions. The singing mistress, Miss Layton, became quite obnoxious with her incessant demands on their throats and a few girls declared a strike and refused to open their mouths at all, only prolonging the agony of those of their classmates who did sing. Those chosen to do readings in church spent

'For your silence,' she said mischevrously.

their dinner breaks rehearsing with the sixth formers. Flora of Miss Sparks' house was the only girl in the first form to be doing anything; she was to sing a small solo.

Games lessons had for some time now taken place indoors and consisted of gymnastics and some exhilarating obstacle courses that Miss Knight invented. Benches were propped up on horses to create a slope to balance up. Then came the parallel bars and the back wall with its wooden climbing bars which had to be traversed before a skipping rope that was kept going by two continuously changing volunteers. The girls would go round and round and have great fun.

Wang Li was as good as her word, teaching Nan a few basic stances and defensive moves. Miss Knight, on observing this tuition going on in a corner of the gymnasium, came over, interested.

'Well, Wang Li, what's this in aid of?' she asked as the two turned guiltily.

'Oh,' Wang Li blushed, 'I was just teaching Nan some Gong Fu.'

'Really? I wonder if you would mind teaching the whole form? I'm sure we would all be interested to learn something new,' invited Miss Knight encouragingly and Wang Li could hardly believe her ears.

'All right,' she muttered, quite overwhelmed and a little nervous of the attitude of the rest of the class.

Porcine Pranks at St. Anne's

She needn't have worried, however, for she was an excellent teacher. She gave a demonstration with a willing victim in the form of Beryl.

'Grab my wrist,' she instructed, and Beryl did so but was thrown off by a twitch of Wang Li's hand.

'Well!' exclaimed a bemused Beryl, 'However did you do that?'

She tried two or three more times but had no success. Her hand just seemed to slide off Wang Li's wrist like butter. The Chinese girl explained how she rolled her hand under and over the attacker's own wrist, forcing them to relinquish their hold.

Next, Wang Li got Beryl to grab onto her in a wrestling hold before swiping her feet from under her, causing her to fall heavily to the thick mat under their feet.

Finally, Wang Li told Beryl to stand out of the way before performing several kicks, the most impressive to the watching girls being one straight up to an imaginary opponent's jaw, effectively doing the splits standing up.

'That is why it is necessary to do the stretches,' she remarked as her classmates and Miss Knight applauded furiously.

What everyone in the first form was hoping for was snow. It had been freezing for several days now and so too cold for snow, but on the Wednesday night the temperature climbed to one degree, and it rained.

When Nan awoke and looked at her little clock it seemed far too light outside. Padding across, she peeked out of the curtains and wonder reflected in her face. The scene that met her eyes was blanketed in a thick powdery covering of snow and large flakes were still swirling out of the papery sky.

Elated, Nan let out a squeak and rushed round, shaking the sleeping forms of the others, 'It's snowing!'

Beryl, for once, raised no objections at being wakened before the dressing bell, and in a matter of seconds everyone was glued to the window.

When Matron arrived on the scene, she had for a miracle no stragglers to keep from falling back asleep. Everyone dressed as quickly as they could, breakfasted so fast that a few of them got stomach-ache and then rushed outside only just remembering hats and coats, scarves and gloves.

Once out in the glistening ne world, the first formers reacted each in their own way. Nan scooped up a gloveful of snow to study, picking out with delight the minuscule individual snowflakes. Barbara stepped heavily off the path cleared by the gardener and waded around in the deep snow, getting her clothes damp as it melted against her. Beryl, predictably, ate a small amount of snow, before pronouncing it cold and bland. Wang li danced around in the fastly falling flakes, turning her face up to the sky to catch them on her tongue and eyelashes. A few got lodged in her dark hair, making her look like a snow queen.

Leonora, meanwhile, wrenched off a clump of fallen snow and compacted it into a ball before hurling it at Elaine. It hit her neck, crumbling on impact and sending a shiver of icy particles down beneath her scarf. 'Oh, Leonora, you mean beast!' she shrieked, stooping to grab a handful of snow which she promptly sent flying towards Leonora. The girl dodged neatly, and it found its mark on Daisy-May instead. Swept away in the heat of the moment, the head girl joined in and soon an all-out war was being waged.

All of a sudden, a figure loomed out of the swirling white and Miss Porter was standing there. Everyone stopped immediately; everyone except Leonora, who was hidden behind a bank of snow. Presently she surged out, hurling a snowball at the place Beryl had been occupying and where the mistress now stood. Realising too late her mistake, Leonora looked on, dismayed as her missile struck her form mistress on the shoulder.

Without even bothering to brush off the snow, Miss Porter bent to compact her own icy ammunition which she launched back at Leonora. Too stunned to dodge, Leonora was caught full in the face to the amusement of her classmates and their form mistress.

'Now to church,' said the mistress firmly, handing Leonora a handkerchief with which to wipe her face, 'There will be plenty of time for playing in the snow at break.'

So the first formers followed Miss Porter through the white carpeted grounds to carol practice, whispered exclamations revealing the general consensus to be that the mistress was in fact a sport.

The snow lessened and gradually stopped falling, but by the first lesson of Geography the girls were still unable to tear their eyes away from the sugar-coated landscape through the window.

'Barbara Wofflespoon! What did I just say?' rapped out Miss Porter wrathfully in one of those bouts of peculiar forgetfulness from which teachers frequently suffer.

Barbara, who had snapped back to attention, was obviously also suffering from the same complaint, 'Umm... something about meanders?' she hazarded, her mind a blank.

"Something' being the operative word?' asked the geography mistress sardonically, 'And meanders is wrong anyway. We were studying them above fifteen minutes ago,' she snapped and then, without enlightening Barbara, continued, 'it's quite obvious that you cannot concentrate. If you wait here quietly, I will ask Miss Montagu if we might have the morning off.'

Porcine Pranks at St. Anne's

As she swept from the room the first formers gazed marvellingly at one another, wondering if they could possibly have heard aright.

When Miss Porter returned, the stampeding on the stairs told its own story; the whole school was to have the morning off to play in the snow.

The first formers made the utmost of it, sallying forth into the crisp white day armed with a wooden sledge they had found propped up against the garden shed next to the woodpile outside the kitchen garden. Locating a suitably sloping hill a few fields away, they took turns to career down two at a time.

'I say! This is super fun!' cried Beryl, her cheeks rosy and her breath coming in little clouds, 'Your turn, Barbara.'

'Thanks,' said Barbara, seating herself behind Elaine, 'Nan,' she added suddenly, 'Wherever's Poppy got to? She was here a minute ago.'

Nan looked around her. Barbara was right; Poppy was nowhere to be seen and yet she had started out with them.

A shout alerted Nan to a presence and, turning, she perceived Poppy jogging up from the path, Bobby lolloping at her heels.

'I couldn't leave her behind,' she explained briefly, 'it's her first snow.'

Snowballs and Philosophy

The piglet explored happily, snuffling the unfamiliar ground and sending snow spraying in all directions. The two girls on the sledge kicked off and sailed down the hill gathering speed before being tipped off by an unseen obstacle beneath the carpeted ground and rolling into the snow.

The two girls on the sledge kicked off and sailed down the hill.

On their way back up to the school, worn out and thirsty after their exercise, the first formers were joined by Amrita and Isobel.

'There you are,' exclaimed the Head Girl, sounding relieved, 'Miss Sparks sent us to fetch you. Everyone's having hot chocolate in the dining hall.' Then, lowering her voice, 'I don't think you were supposed to stray from the school grounds, you know.'

Everyone exchanged guilty looks and Daisy-May closed her eyes in dismay. How was it that they always seemed to be getting into trouble; this time she hadn't even suspected that they were in it.

'We'll say we found you in the woods by the stables,' suggested Amrita with a sidelong glance at her fellow sixth former, 'We'll have to pass by there in any case to put Bobby back.'

The first formers agreed gratefully to this plan of campaign and the little group set off, led by the two older girls, and with everyone petting Bobby all the while. Amrita even took a biscuit from her coat pocket and offered it to the animal. As she did so the white light caught the silver bangle at her wrist making it glint.

'What is that?' asked Nan curiously.

'This?' Amrita indicated the metal bangle and Nan nodded, 'this is my Kara, my steel bracelet. It's a symbol of my faith as a Sikh.'

'This?' Amrita indicated the metal bangle and Nan nodded.

'Oh, does Miss Montagu make you come to church, then?' cried Nan, outraged.

'Nobody makes me come to church,' Amrita assured her, amused, 'I come because I like the gothic building and the colours of the stained glass and the vaulted ceiling. And although I may not be Christian, I don't deny the validity of other religions as many other faiths do. Sikhs believe that all faiths are a reflection of the same thing only seen through the eyes of different cultures.'

Everyone had been listening intently, 'That makes sense,' Poppy said now, 'I'm not particularly religious, but we know so little about the world really. I mean it must have come from something.'

'You're very philosophical this morning,' laughed Beryl, 'What did you have for breakfast?'

'Porridge, but I have that every morning.'

'You sound like Voltaire,' observed Wang Li unexpectedly.

'Why? Did he have porridge for breakfast?' queried Barbara lightly.

'No!' laughed Wang Li, 'He was a deist. He didn't believe in the church of the time, but he believed in God as the architect of the world. Only he didn't believe God could interfere in events on Earth.'

'Well, that sounds sensible. I mean, if they could, there wouldn't be any bad in the world, would there, and there's plenty of that,' observed Poppy, still showing unusual sagacity.

'Who is Voltaire?' Elaine wanted to know.

'He was a French philosopher in the eighteenth century,' supplied Wang Li fluently.

'How on Earth do you know all this Wang Li?' exclaimed Barbara, 'You're like a human encyclopaedia!'

'Mamzelle has been lending me some books in French to read,' explained Wang Li heavily.

'And you've been reading them?' this from Nan, 'Well done!' A sudden thought stuck Nan. Of course, Wang Li was probably not Christian either, but she had never really thought about what religion the Chinese girl followed. She felt a little guilty for never questioning her. 'What do you believe in, Wang Li?' she asked now, hesitantly.

'Oh!' Wang Li flung expressive arms in the air, 'I don't know. My people are part Daoist, part Buddhist, but we follow a bit of everything really. I think Gong Fu is my faith.'

'I thought you all followed the teachings of Confucius,' remarked Beryl, a tad insensitively.

'Kong Zi? Oh, no, not all of us, although of course, he is a big name in China. Personally, I prefer Lao Zi.'

'And people say first formers are shrimps of the first water!' cried Isobel, a note of awe in her voice, 'Come on, everyone, inside or you'll miss out on that hot chocolate!'

25

Until Next Term

The snow hung around over the next few days, gradually melting down to a sloshy consistency. That last weekend was spent mostly in the village tea shop and around the common room fire playing games. Miss Porter had relented so Leonora went as well, although she insisted she would have gone anyway.

School finished on the Wednesday afternoon before parents arrived for the carol concert in the evening. Faces gleaming with scrubbed cleanliness, uniforms immaculate, the girls' sweet voices filled the gothic interior of the church enchanting the spellbound listeners. Hundreds of candles, each contributing a small warm glow picked out the various holy colours of the stained glass and cast flickering shadows on the stone walls. The magical atmosphere was only heightened when large fluffy flakes were seen to be swirling down from the heavens.

As soon as Miss Montagu had said her final piece and signalled her willingness for people to start departing there was a perfect rush for the heavy wooden door. Miss Sparks thoughtfully propped it open before standing back to observe the progress of the rabble with an occasional 'whoa there, Appleby' 'Not so fast, Forsyth' and 'Not you as well Brain'. Daisy-May skidded to an abrupt halt and continued at a more sedate pace.

Barbara and her father dashed out to join the others in marvelling at the perfect blizzard outside, but Poppy was stuck to her aunt who was trying to engage Miss Porter in a serious conversation about the term's work.

Nan, spotting her friend's predicament, tugged at her father's sleeve. 'Might we invite Poppy for a few days during the Christmas hols, please?'

'Of course,' answered Mr Miller readily, then, taking in the situation, strode over and detached Miss Blake skilfully from her niece. Poppy's aunt coloured slightly, quite overcome with this unexpected attention, and had soon forgotten all about Poppy and Miss Porter and was strolling through the grounds chatting amicably with Nan's parents.

Nan stepped up and took Poppy's arm. 'I say!' she said as they followed the slowly dispersing crowd back

Porcine Pranks at St. Anne's

to St. Anne's, 'Would you like to spend part of the hols with us? Father said you might.'

Poppy stopped and stared at her friend in delight, 'Would I?' she echoed, 'You bet I would!'

The next morning- the last morning that they would wake up at St. Anne's for three weeks- was, as always, chaotic. Trunks were brought out from the box rooms and girls flew about in a state of wild excitement, piling in clothes and books, teddies and toiletries, all the while keeping up several different conversations at once.

'I say Poppy, those are my stockings you're so diligently packing!' cried Barbara, 'Honestly, I hope to Goodness you haven't torn them!'

'And Beryl!' exclaimed a vexed Daisy-May, 'That's my trunk you've got, you idiot!'

'Is it? Oh, so it is. Blow! What a pity; I'd about finished packing it!'

'Has anyone seen my clock?' demanded Elaine, 'I put it down somewhere for five seconds and now I can't find it anywhere!'

'Is this it, Elaine?' asked Barbara, holding aloft the missing article.

'Yes! Oh, wherever did you find it?'

'On top of the washbasin of all places; you really are a chump, Elaine.'

At long last, everyone seemed to be packed up and ready to go. Gardeners and groundsmen filed in to carry the heavy trunks downstairs and outside to where parents were waiting to stow them into automobiles.

For the very first time, Elaine was not to spend her holidays roaming around an empty boarding school with only a handful of students, mistresses and staff for company. Instead, she was to join Barbara and her father who were off up to Scotland for a week before taking up their residence in the grounds of St. Becket's.

Daisy-May was to accompany Beryl for two weeks at her family's townhouse in London. Wang Li and her parents were to get the ferry to France and then the train into the Swiss Alps where they planned to go skiing. Wang Li was so excited that she tripped down the last couple of steps and her hat came flying off. Nan who was nearby and had witnessed the spectacle picked it up and handed it back to her.

'Xiè xiè, thank you.'

'Méi guān xì,' replied Nan startling her friend with her correct pronunciation, 'Don't forget to write, will you?'

'I'll send you a postcard!' promised the girl, climbing into the waiting car, 'Zài jiàn! See you next term!'

Nan waved until she was out of sight and then picked up her night case and Lacrosse stick and weaved her way through the emotional greetings to where her parents were waiting in their car.

Porcine Pranks at St. Anne's

Behind her Mamzelle Meuhourat was clinging to Beryl and seemed in danger of never releasing her. Miss Porter stood to one side with Miss Sparks, waving.

'So, your first term at St. Anne's,' Mrs Miller was saying, turning round in her seat to talk to Nan as she made sure that she was tightly tucked up underneath the travelling rugs, 'How was it?'

'Marvellous,' breathed Nan, 'I can't wait to be back, though I shall enjoy the hols as well!' She thought back over all the exciting things that had happened that term. Tricks on Mamzelle, a midnight feast, scoring the winning goal in a Lacrosse match, a snowball fight and a secret mission to put a pig in a mistress' bedroom! That was one highlight she probably wouldn't be telling her parents about! Gracious, she wondered just what fun she would get up to next term!

Twisting around, her face glued to the square back window, Nan watched until the school was out of sight. Her last glimpse of it revealed Poppy and one of her elder brothers who had come to fetch her, bundling Bobby the pig into the back seat of a rickety old open top car.

Maps, plans and glossary...

Porcine Pranks at St. Anne's

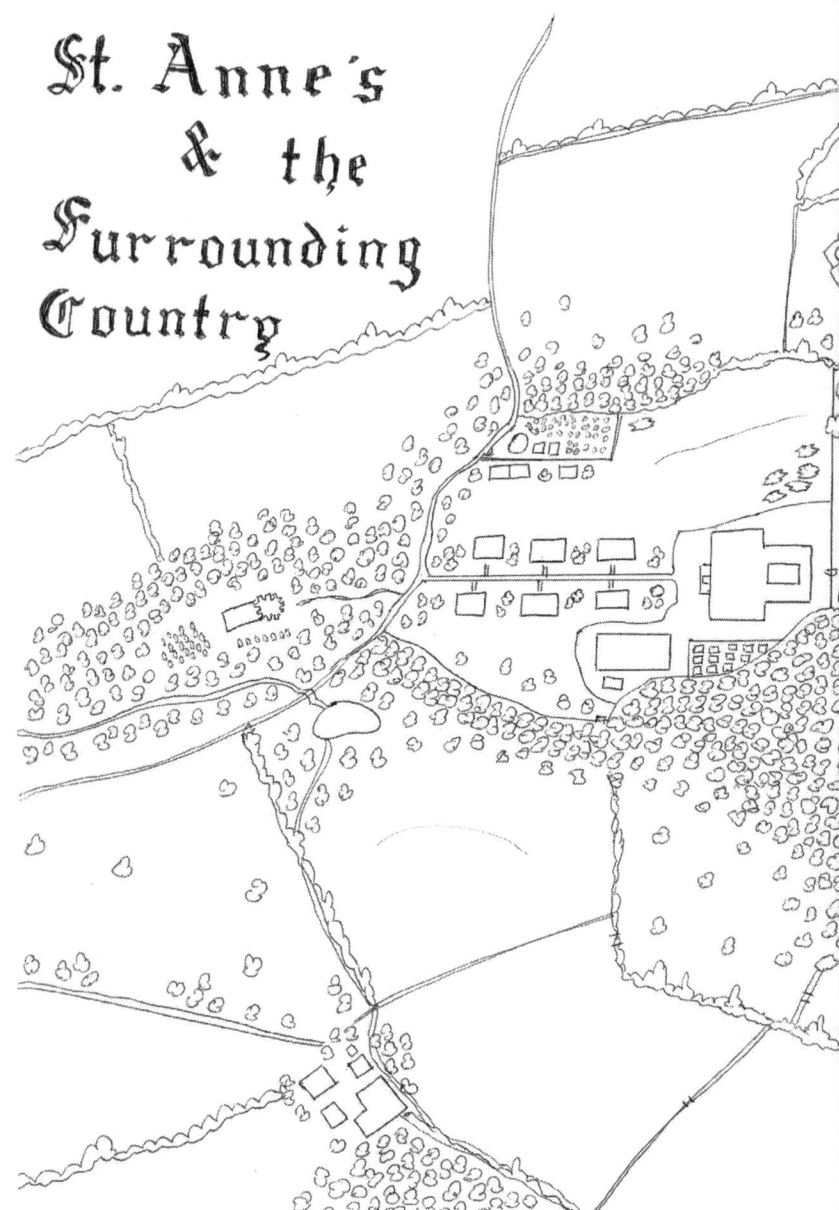

St. Anne's
& the
Surrounding
Country

Maps, plans and glossary...

First form timetable

	7:45	8:15	9:00	11		1:30		3:05	4:35	5:30	6
Monday		B R	French Mlle Meuhourat	B	Science Miss Sparks	History Miss Knight	L	Latin Miss Montagu	Prep.	Free time	T
Tuesday		E A	Maths Miss Porter	R	English Miss Porter	Sewing Miss Whyte	U	Games Miss Knight	Prep.	Free time	
Wednesday		K F	Art Miss Whyte	E	Drama Miss Winter	Maths Miss Porter	N	French Mlle Leroy	Prep.	Free time	E
Thursday		A S	Geography Miss Porter	A	Music Miss Layton	French Mlle Leroy	C	Games Miss Knight	Prep.	Free time	
Friday		T	History Miss Knight	K	Science Miss Sparks	French Mlle Meuhourat	H	Geography Miss Porter	Prep.	Free time	A

Maps, plans and glossary...

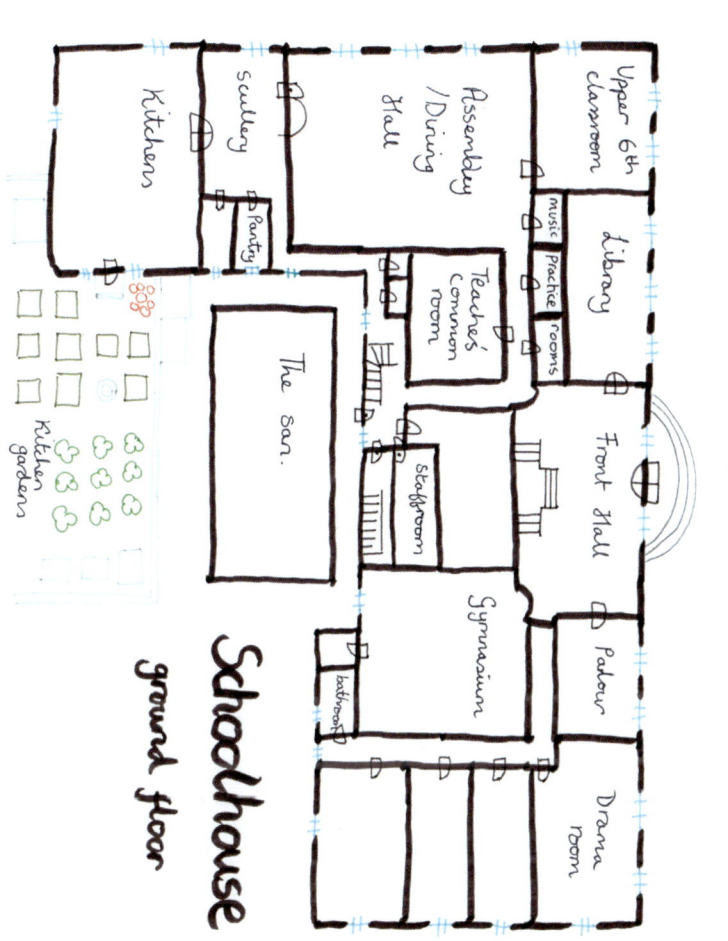

Maps, plans and glossary...

Plan 3

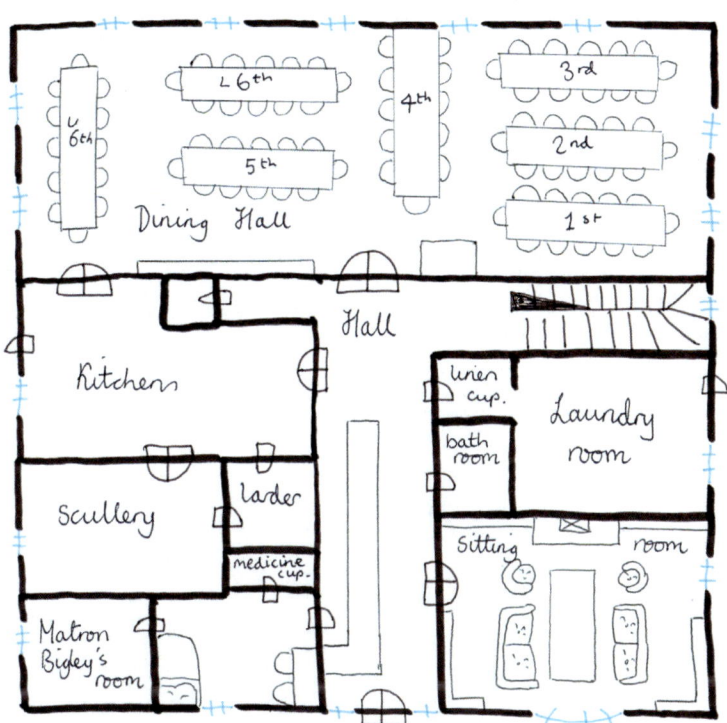

Mrs Porter's Boarding house
ground floor

Plan 4

Min Porter's Boarding house 1st floor

Glossary

French:

Bonsoir, mes enfants
- good evening, my children

Ça suffit
- that is enough

La pauvre fille
- the poor girl

Bonjour, mes enfants
- good morning, my children

Mais oui
- but yes

Porcine Pranks at St. Anne's

Ce n'est pas difficile
- it is not difficult

Et avant ça vous habitiez en chine, n'est-pas, ma chérie ?
- and before that you lived in China, did you not, my dear?

C'est vraiment fou, n'est pas ?
- it is truly mad, is it not?

C'est tellement épouvantable ce qu'elle subit !
- it is really awful how she suffers

Ah, non, je ne sais pas
- oh, no, I don't know

Merci bien ma chère Beryl
- thank you very much my dear Beryl

Tiens !
- (exclamation)

Ah non, ce n'est pas vrai, ça !
- oh no, it is not true, that!

Mon Dieu
- my God

Glossary

Nom d'un nom d'un nom...
- name of a name of a name... (exclamation)

Méchante fille
- naughty girl

Tu fais vraiment des bêtises, hein ?
- you are really up to mischief, aren't you?

Tais-toi !
- shut up!

Ma petite
- my little one

Eh bien
- very well

La neige, c'était tellement belle !
- the snow, it was beautiful!

Alors
- now then

Allons-y
- come on

Porcine Pranks at St. Anne's

La lecture
- the reading

Il y eut une rafale de vent glaciale et la fenêtre se referma avec un coup de cœur arrêtant
- there was a glacial gust of wind and the window shut itself with a heart stopping bang

C'est bon
- all is well

Tout fut tranquille. Soudain il y eut un terrible gémissement de la cheminée et une pluie de suie jaillit
- everything was quiet. Suddenly there came a terrible wailing from the chimney and a plume of soot fell down

Qu'est ce qui se passe ?
- what is happening?

On se trouve dans une école hantée
- we are in a haunted school

Ce n'est pas joli, ça !
- it is not nice, that!

Tu as raison
- you are right

Glossary

Oh, la, la
- (exclamation)

La belle langue française
- the beautiful French language

Toute l'après-midi
- all afternoon

Être
- the verb to be

Ce que j'ai fait pendant les vacances d'été
- what I did during the summer holidays

Ma tête
- my head

Bonne nuit
- good night

C'est égal
- it doesn't matter

Chambre de lit
- bedroom

Porcine Pranks at St. Anne's

Mignonne
- cute

Un sanglier
- a wild boar

Oui, c'est ça
- yes, that is it

Oui, bien sûr
- yes, of course

C'était tellement étonnant
- it was very astonishing

En fait
- in fact

Au naturel
- naked

Latin:

Unde veniunt filii tui?
- where do your brothers come from?

Filii mei ab Germania veniunt
- my brothers come from Germany

Glossary

Mandarin Chinese:

Although simplified Chinese characters and pinyin romanisation were only introduced in the 1950s in China, I am using them here because they are more useful to a modern student of Mandarin Chinese.

功夫
- gōngfū
Kung-fu

你好
- nǐhǎo
Hello

不错
- bùcuò
Not bad

老唐
- lǎotáng
Old Tang

小熊猫
- xiǎoxióngmāo
Little panda

Porcine Pranks at St. Anne's

老师
- lǎoshī
Teacher

可爱
- kě'ài
Cute

猪肉
- zhūròu
Pork

妈妈
- māma
Mother

爸爸
- bàba
Father

不客气
- bùkèqì
You're welcome

孔子
- kǒngzǐ
Confucius

老子
- lǎozǐ
Lao Zi

谢谢
- xièxiè
Thank you

没关系
- méiguānxì
Don't worry

再见
- zàijiàn
See you again

About the author

I am the author of the St. Anne's school series. When not writing and drawing, I enjoy learning languages including French, German, Mandarin Chinese, Italian, Ukrainian, and Japanese as well as practicing Tai Chi, Karate and the piano.